# Arvid's Treasure

Cover photo by Len Nasman

An out-of-work writer finds adventure, danger, and romance as he searches for treasure hidden by his Great Uncle Arvid somewhere in the Colorado mountains.

# Table of Contents

## Chapter 1 - Aunt Annie Olofsson

Annie was pouring fresh coffee into her next door neighbor's cup. Martha and Annie had been having coffee nearly every morning for over 20 years, ever since they became neighbors. Annie lived in the house that her grandfather Olof Jonsson had built in the 1860's, nearly a hundred years ago.

The weather that morning in Basking Ridge, NJ was mild for early June, so they were having their morning gossip session out on the summer porch.

"Annie, did you say that your nephew Andrew was fired from his job?"

"No, not fired. Laid off. Or, whatever you call it when your company shuts down. I'm not sure what Andrew will do now. At least he shouldn't have any money worries for a while. He hasn't done much but ride the train to his Manhattan job back and forth for the last few years since he graduated from college. And I've never known him to throw his money around. A couple of years ago, when his parents were killed in that terrible car accident, he sold the family house in upstate New York and put all of the money in some kind of Mutual Fund or something. A lot of kids his age would have bought a fancy car and maybe rented a better apartment. Andrew just seemed to close himself in from the world. He even dumped that girl he was seeing.

"I talked to Andrew on the phone yesterday and he promised to visit me soon. You can be sure I'll quiz him about his plans, and I might have a suggestion or two for him. A young boy like that needs to get away and get his mind off that old job. Maybe take some time for a change of scenery. Travel a bit."

"Now Annie, I know you have had a bee in your bonnet for years to get Andrew interested in your Uncle Arvid's Colorado buried treasure. I hope you're not going to try and send him off on *that* wild goose chase."

"Well, whether there is anything to that old family legend or not, it would certainly force him to see a little of the country while he is still young enough to climb a mountain or two and learn about people and places outside of a sterile New York City office building."

"Come on now, Annie! That's not quite fair! He had lots of assignments for that *Tales, Trails, and Tails* magazine. Are you sure that you're not just a little bored around here and want to at least vicariously share some adventure in your life?"

6

"Well, a young fellow like Andrew shouldn't be satisfied just following the progress of hikers, or chasing bikers, or writing about the differences between black squirrels and gray squirrels. He needs to get out more in the world, experience new places and people. Maybe even sew a few wild oats."

"OK Annie, but don't be too hard on him. And when he comes by, be sure to give him my love."

# Arvid's Treasure

## Chapter 2 - Andrew Olofsson

While Aunt Annie and her friend were talking about him, Andrew was sitting in his apartment thinking about what he should do with his life now that *Tales, Trails and Tails* was shutting down. Maybe he had stayed in this place a little too long. He'd first rented it when he was a student at Fairleigh Dickinson University and had held on to it long after he graduated.

Early in his student days he'd lucked into this furnished basement apartment in a private home near the campus. It had a separate entrance, a bedroom, a kitchen-living room, a bathroom and an adequate storage area. It was convenient to the campus, and after he graduated and went to work for *Tales, Trails, and Tails* magazine, he could get on a train at either Convent or Madison Station for an easy commute to the city.

He felt comfortable in his apartment; it had been his only home for several years now. It was close to anything a student, or a former student, could want. After his parents were killed in that awful car accident, he received a generous settlement from the trucking company whose driver was responsible for the crash. As an only child, he also inherited the family home back in Ithaca, New York. where his parents had been on the faculty for many years at Cornell.

His former girl friend was more interested in big city life then he was, and this was one of the differences that finally drove them apart. That, and his frequent assignments for TT,&T that took him for extended trips following hikers on trails like the Appalachian, North Country, and other popular trails in the north east. He also was assigned to write stories about long distance bicycle rides, and occasional nature or wildlife stories that kept him away from the city, sometimes for weeks at a time.

One of his favorite assignments had been to do a series of articles on Tom Brown Jr. who had a reputation for finding lost people. Eventually Brown founded a Tracker School based on the teachings of Stalking Wolf, the Apache elder Tom had first met when he was just seven years old. Brown published a long list of stories and books about how he has used his skills to locate lost children, criminals, and to get up very close to wild animals.

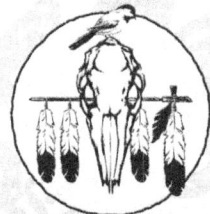

TRACKER SCHOOL
Tracking, Nature and Wilderness Survival School

The school had classes in tracking, survival skills, and the philosophy of how to be at one with nature. After the initial magazine article assignment, Andrew visited Tom Brown several times and learned about the almost mystical experiences of getting close to nature.

After spending too much time in this introspective mood, he reminded himself of his promise to visit his Aunt Annie.

# Arvid's Treasure

## Chapter 3 - Jane Rutherfield

Jane Rutherfield had just spent several days visiting her college friend Janice. After graduating from Colorado State University, Janice had attended Northwestern University, majoring in fashion design. Jane had stayed at CSU and received a Master's Degree in Wildlife Management. During the visit, it soon became apparent to Jane that although she and Janice had been the best of friends in their undergraduate days, their lives had gone in very different directions.

Janice invited Jane to a party with some of Janice's fashion design friends, and it was soon obvious to Jane that Janice's lifestyle had changed dramatically since their days at Colorado State. In those days, it was not unusual for them on an occasional weekend to attend keggers where a group would bring a couple of kegs of beer to some mountain meadow, drink a little, party a lot, do a bit of necking, sleep it off, and get back to their studies when the weekend was over.

The party in Chicago was much wilder than a Colorado kegger. Jane disappointed Janice by refusing to smoke unlabeled cigarettes, join in jello shot or other drinking games, and resist being picked up by guys with wandering hands. After the party, Janice told Jane that she was out of touch, and needed to "get with it," whatever that meant. Janice suggested Jane was square, a prude, old fashioned, afraid to let loose, not liberated, and probably would never be found attractive to men. Janice also had unfavorable things to say about Jane's sense of fashion.

Jane tried to share the excitement Janice felt about the latest fashions and designs. Janice tried to convince her that the 1960's were the start of a new fashion era, and that Jane needed to 'get with the program' and update her wardrobe. Janice even gifted Jane a frilly blouse and mini skirt, and even added some Frederick's of Hollywood underwear and a pair of spike heels. Jane didn't want to start a fight about the wardrobe selections, so she humored her and wore the new outfit to the train station where she bid Janice an emotional goodbye.

The spike heels made it hard to drag her big red suitcase through the station and across the platform to the train. At one point, when the suitcase got snagged on a curb, she gave a mighty pull, her spike heel slipped, she lost her

14

balance, and fell against a man whose quick reaction kept her from sprawling across the platform. She was embarrassed, regained her balance, and continued without thanking the man who stopped her fall. She silently cursed herself for allowing Janice to select her clothes for the day, and kept dragging her suitcase to the train.

As the train headed out of Chicago's Union Station toward Colorado, Jane sadly realized that friends can drift apart and go off in completely different directions. She was annoyed by the thought that Janice considered her a prude. As her mini skirt kept riding up, she also thought about how much more comfortable she would be wearing her usual jeans and shirts than wearing Janice's idea of the latest women's fashions. She accepted the fact that she was, and probably always would be, a western girl.

Jane was born and raised in Colorado. Her grandparents operated the Diamond Bar ranch in northern Colorado that was originally homesteaded by their parents. The ranch land was part of land deeded by the government to a railroad company that then sold land to fund the construction of the first transcontinental railroad. As a result, the land on both sides of the railroad right of way was a patchwork quilt of alternating government and private sections of land.

Many ranchers took advantage of the alternate government sections and grazed cattle on much larger areas than they actually owned.

Even after Jane's parents settled in Denver in good, stable, business jobs, Jane spent a lot more time on the ranch then she did in the city. When it was time to pick a college, she never considered the University of Colorado. Colorado State was the Land Grant University and remained true to it's Aggie roots. CU had the reputation as a party school in spite of some very advanced physics and technology programs. While student unrest, 'hippie behavior,' and demonstrations became common at CU, CSU students were more likely to be seen in clothes that would fit in at rodeos. In the 1960's, the Vet Medicine students at Colorado State were still wearing white shirts and ties to class.

The Rocky Mountains were deeply ingrained in Jane's blood. Her decision to major in Wildlife Management was undoubtedly influenced by her Uncle Bill who wrote his Master's Thesis on the behavior of beavers. Bill worked for the Colorado Parks and Wildlife Headquarters Fort Collins Office. Jane had often tagged along with Uncle Bill when he was on duty at Game Check Stations, habitat studies, or at annual Wing Dings when hunters brought in wings from legally killed migratory game birds for analysis.

As the train headed toward Colorado, Jane realized that the frilly women's clothes that Janice had insisted she wear were much too uncomfortable. So she grabbed her big red suitcase and headed to the train toilet to change into something more comfortable. The sooner she could shed Janice's 'fashionable' outfit, the better.

Arvid's Treasure

## Chapter 4 - Dr. Tex Frey

After 18 holes of golf, Dr. Tex Frey was approached by Jim Rogers in the locker room; Jim asked Tex if he was planning any new hunting trips to Colorado.

"There is usually something in the works. Are you interested in doing a little hunting?"

"Yes, I've heard some of the guys at the club talk about the great trips you've arranged for them,"

"Why don't you come over to my house for drinks around eight o'clock this evening; I'll tell you about some of our hunting successes."

Tex had taken on the name Tex shortly after moving his dermatology practice from New York to Texas. Like most folks from the north, he quickly discovered there was a significant disadvantage in Texas if there was any hint of a 'Yankee' background. So Tex added an expensive hat and boots to his wardrobe, and worked hard at removing any hint of New York from his speech.

Tex, whose actual name was Dr. Moses Friedberg, came from a long line of northeastern physicians. His father practiced at Mount Sinai for many years, and several uncles were also in the medical business. Friedberg (aka Frey) was more interested in his investment portfolio than he was in providing life saving services to the community. While in medical school, he determined that dermatology provided a comfortable and reliable income stream without the demands on general practitioners, or the intense pressure and responsibilities of specialized surgeons. Before moving to Texas, Friedberg changed his name from Moses Friedberg to Mark Frey. He made sure that all of his medical certificates reflected the name change.

Frey enjoyed the 'good ol' boy' southern country club culture. He liked the ladies, and he liked to brag about his hunting trips to the Colorado mountains. Of course, his eastern suburban and Ivy League upbringing did very little to prepare him for the rigors of hunting in the mountain back country. In his mind, however, he could have been a model for the original 'Marlboro Man'. His trips included participating in some serious poker games. In a backroom card game in Trinidad, Colorado, he made some contacts who knew where, for a price, hunting trophies could be acquired. Dr. Tex had provided several of his Texas friends with some nice macho looking wall hangings.

When Jim Rogers arrived that evening, Tex invited him into the great room of his Wichita Falls, Texas McMansion. Near the ceiling at one end of the 18 foot high great room was a large mounted trophy mule deer head. He and another country club friend had nearly finished a large pitcher of 'Death in the Afternoon' a favorite drink among an insider golfing group.

Jim Rogers gazed at the deer head and remarked; "Tex, I've always admired that magnificent trophy. There are rumors around the clubhouse that you know where to pick up one of those things for a price, you know what I mean."

Dr. Tex did indeed know. What was a not very closely guarded secret among a small group of golf buddies was that the guys who accompanied Tex on Colorado hunting trips were remarkably successful in acquiring elk, bighorn sheep, mule deer, antelope, or other trophies that could be bragged about while sharing drinks with friends.

"You realize these Colorado hunting trips can be fairly expensive." Tex replied with a smile.

"If you can guarantee success, I don't think the cost would be an issue."

"Oh, I can guarantee success all right. Why don't you do some thinking about just how much it would be

worth to you to have a nice trophy of your own. Maybe
we can get together again some time and work out the
details of a hunt."

"I think I'll just do that, and be back in touch with
you."

Tex showed Rogers out and then went back to his
great room, finished off another glass of 'Death in the
Afternoon,' sat back, and laughed to himself about
how easy it was to squeeze money out of these Texas
country club fools. At as much as $40,000 for a
hunting trip and a trophy for the country club
millionaires, Tex was feeling pretty good and keeping
his bank account full.

## Chapter 5 - Death of a Magazine

Friday evening Andrew was sitting on his gliding rocker, and reviewing the events of the day. Just before lunch time Silas Redfern, the owner of TT&T had called the staff together for an announcement. Rumors had been floating around for a couple of weeks that the owner was considering retirement. As a result, there was a lot of speculation about what would happen to the company. Now it was official. The owner was indeed retiring.

When Silas formally announced his retirement, he also said he had several offers from different companies interested in buying the magazine. He referred to those companies as vulture capitalists who bought a company, stripped the assets over a period of months, or maybe a year or two, and then declared bankruptcy. He wasn't going to let that happen to his company and employees. Instead he planned to liquidate TT&T and then share the value of the assets with the employees in the form of

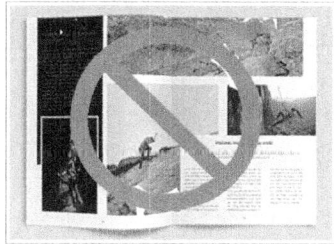

severance pay. He also would provide letters of reference to anyone who made a request.

During the following two weeks, all work on the current (last) issue of TT&T would be completed, regular pay checks would be issued, and within a month, severance checks would be issued.

Although the closing of the magazine had been rumored for a while, no one had guessed how it would end. Feelings among the employees were mixed. No one was happy to lose their job, but no one could complain about the way they were being treated.

Now, with the magazine closing, Andrew felt a little lost, but also a kind of freedom. Maybe it was time to try and practice some of the philosophy he'd learned from the Tom Brown tracker school. Perhaps it was time to try something new. Maybe he had let himself get too comfortable living like an aging college student; perhaps it was time to move on, but move on to what?

Andrew gave Aunt Annie a call, and made an appointment to visit her on Sunday.

## Chapter 6 - Aunt Annie's Treasure Tale

Annie Olofsson removed the last batch of Toll House cookies from the oven and set them out to cool. Ever since Andrew was a little boy, she always had a jar full of cookies waiting for him. She had tried to keep even closer to Andrew since the dreadful car crash that killed his parents. Andrew was an only child and Annie felt since she was the only real family he had, it was her job to look after Andrew and provide him with occasional advice and guidance, and cookies.

Meanwhile, Andrew got his 10 speed bike out of his storage area, and set off on a ride through the familiar New Jersey countryside. It was about a dozen miles from his Madison, NJ apartment to Aunt Annie's in Basking Ridge. He got an early start and took time to follow Long Hill Road through part of the Great Swamp. Taking a little break from pedaling, he walked for a while along a wooden boardwalk built for people to see a bit of the swamp. Most of the

25

swamp was nearly impossible to explore on foot, and it was surprising to find a place in one of the most densely populated states where wildlife and exotic plants thrived. As he walked along the boardwalk, frogs hopped and dove into the shallow water, birds scolded from above, and a 6 foot long blacksnake raced through the brush and up a tree. Here, in the middle of New Jersey, was a quiet nature refuge. It was a good place to relax and be distracted from the worries about what direction his life should take now that he was soon to be out of a job.

Annie's Basking Ridge house had been in the family for several generations. Annie inherited the house from her father and mother Karl and Marta Olofsson, and they had inherited it from her grandparents Olof and Katryn Jonsson. Olof Jonsson was a hard working carpenter who immigrated from Sweden and was successful enough to eventually build, and later expand the Basking Ridge house. Annie didn't own a car, and the space in the garage with its partial loft still had a collection of tools and memorabilia that had accumulated over the years.

One item that Annie had retrieved in anticipation of Andrew's visit was a small metal box that had been sent from Colorado by Andrew's great-great uncle, Arvid Jonsson. The tin box came with instructions that

it was very valuable and had to be be saved for him until his return.

Arvid was one of those family characters who was never able to settle down and act normal. He was a dreamer and schemer. He had immigrated to the US from Sweden with a vision of somehow striking it rich.

When word of gold discoveries in Colorado hit the news in the late 1850's, Arvid decided to head west. After the mysterious treasure box from Colorado arrived, Arvid was never heard from again. It was assumed he was dead. The family speculated he was killed by Indians, or in a gold camp gun fight, or more likely in a train wreck; train wrecks were very common in those days. In any case, the box was a family mystery. It was once opened by Arvid's nephew, Nils Olofsson. Nils discovered a crude finger sized silver ingot and a collection of notes which he translated from Swedish to English. Nils died young in the early 1900's and never lived to follow up on the mystery. The box was left on a shelf and nearly forgotten until Annie accidentally discovered it when she was rearranging things in the garage She moved it to a shelf in the dining room with a few other family knickknacks. Annie decided it was just the thing to stimulate

Andrew's curiosity and push him to new adventures and experiences.

Andrew parked his bike on Annie's front porch and could smell fresh baked cookies through the screen door. He knocked on the door, and Annie shouted through the screen for him to come on in. He took his regular place at the kitchen table and soon found a cold glass of milk and a plate full of fresh cookies in front of him. Annie told him she had read about the closing of TT&T in the New York Times. Andrew filled her in on details of the closing of the company by Silas Redfern, the owner of TT&T, and the generous settlement provided to the employees. Andrew then settled back and waited for the anticipated quizzing about his future plans.

Annie said, "Let me tell you a little about your family history. You know that I am your father's sister. For reasons that I won't bother you with, I never married, that story is not important. Our parents were Karl and Marta Olofsson. Marta was a Jonsson before she married your Grandpa Karl, who met her at a Swede dance. She was an orphan and came to America when she was 18 years old to work as a maid for a rich Swedish family in Brooklyn. Karl, like his father before him, was an excellent carpenter.

"Karl's father, your great grandfather, was named Olof Jonsson. Olof's father was Jon Andersson. In the old days in Sweden, children were given the names of their fathers. Thus Jon Andersson's son was Olof Jonsson, and Olof Jonsson's son was named Karl Olofsson. The old Swedish surname convention eventually died out and the family stuck with the name Olofsson. Otherwise, you would be named Andrew Jonsson instead of Olofsson. By the way, girls were named the same way. Jon Andersson's daughter was named Annie Jonsdotter until she married.

"Anyway, Your great grand father, Olof Jonsson, had a brother, Arvid Jonsson. Arvid followed his brother from Sweden, but instead of settling down with a trade like Olof, Arvid was a dreamer. He imagined himself getting rich quick in America and dreamed of going back to Sweden as a very wealthy man. He tried a number of get rich quick schemes and usually ended up back here begging money from his brother. Eventually, he headed west with the idea of striking it rich in Colorado. One day a small metal box arrived in the mail from Arvid. He wrote Olof that the contents of the box were very valuable, and some day were going to make them all rich.

"Arvid the dreamer was never heard from again. The family finally assumed he was dead. The old box gathered dust on a shelf until it was discovered by your Uncle Nils. In the box, Nils found a rough, crudely made little finger sized silver ingot and a stack of papers hand written in Swedish. The first page had *Arvid Jonssons underbara resa genom America.*

"The box also contained what looked like a map. Nils translated the pages, but unfortunately, Nils died before he got around to trying to follow the map to Arvid's treasure.

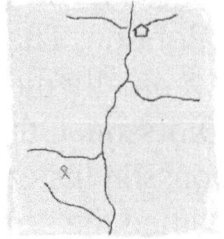

"I suspect you assumed I would be asking you what your plans are now that your job at TT&T has ended." Annie said, "I'm sure you're probably wondering what you should do now that you are all grown up.

"Here is my advice. You now have some time to do a little exploring. You've become a little too comfortable; you've never quite gotten out of the easy student life style. Sure, you've been going off to work every day, and earned your keep. You've been taking on assignments at TT&T and getting good marks and reviews for the work you've done... just like a good college student. But you're still living like a college student, in the same town, and even in the same apartment.

"The closing of TT&T, and the fact that you don't really have any money worries, has provided you with an opportunity few people ever enjoy. So get out there. Discover some new worlds. Take Arvid's tin box and map and search for his treasure. The chances are that there is no treasure, or that it is impossible to find. But the hunt will get you out of your comfort zone. You may just find something in your life that's better than simply sitting in your student apartment forever.

"There, I've spoken! Now have your cookies and milk!"

With that she pushed the old tin box across the table, and Andrew meekly said, "Thanks Aunt Annie," and picked it up.

Andrew tried hard to ride his bicycle back to Madison without losing concentration and ending up in a ditch in the middle of the Great Swamp. He had too many things to sort out. First, there was the process of spending the next two weeks helping to close down TT&T. He only had one active project, and that was pretty much completed. Maybe a couple more proof reads, then off to the layout guy for integrating graphics, then to the editor for the final polishing. The rest of the time would be spent mostly doing grunt work: cleaning out his desk, helping the staff clear out cabinets, and packing boxes.

Then, there was the issue of trying to determine where his career should go next. He needed to update his resume and decide where he might apply for a new job. He needed to decide what companies he might be interested in, or what companies might be interested in him. It would be hard to find a company with a better boss then Silas had been. He doubted that there would be very many executives who would show employees as much respect and support as the owner of TT&T.

What about just going freelance? He certainly had enough money to live on no matter how long it took to develop contacts. However, the idea of having to make new contacts, act as a salesman for every new project, and then run the gauntlet of submitting work to editorial boards was not very appealing.

And, then there was Aunt Annie's crazy idea of going on some wild goose chase treasure hunt to Colorado. He had never been there. Facing the unknown is always a little scary. He believed that he was a pretty good researcher, so maybe he should attack the idea just the way he attacked most new writing projects. What was Colorado like in the days that Uncle Arvid set out on his own adventure into the unknown? What did Arvid's map show? Could he possibly locate the place after so many years had passed?

At least he had time now to do some research. His first step would be the Fairleigh Dickinson University Library. As an alumnus, he still had library privileges. Since he still had two weeks to help close up TT&T, he could also take advantage of the New York Public Library. If he couldn't find what he needed in the second largest library in the United States, it probably didn't exist.

Also, he recalled that the staff photographer at TT&T, Farley McFarland, had covered several stories in Colorado. He invited Farley for dinner at Mama Leone's so he could quiz him about Colorado. No one ever refused an invitation to Mama Leone's.

Mamma Leone's
FAMOUS DINNER
SERVED ONLY UNTIL MIDNIGHT

## Chapter 7 - Dinner with Farley

Mama Leone's had been a favorite of locals and tourists since it opened in 1906. Now, nearly 6 decades later, it still maintained the original ambiance and many of the traditional menu selections. Andrew met Farley there after a busy day at TT&T. They chatted about the company closing, and reminisced about some of their best and worst projects and experiences. After a little of this chit chat, Farley said, "OK, Andrew, I doubt that you invited me to dinner just to pass the time of day. What's the real agenda here?"

"You're right, of course," replied Andrew. "I've heard you've spent time in Colorado and since I'm thinking of making a trip there, I'm hoping you can offer some advice."

"Just what kind of advice? I'm not a travel agent. There are a lot of travel agencies all around the area that can help you."

"No, I'm not interested in tourist kinds of stuff. I've heard stories you've had some interesting experiences out there, and I'm looking for information beyond the regular tourist kind of thing."

"Do you want to know about my life as a ski bum? I've done a little of that. I spent a couple of winters on the ski patrol at Breckenridge. Had to give that up because of an injury I got jumping off a cliff for a Warren Miller ski movie.

"Are you thinking about climbing the Diamond on Long's Peak? I've done a little technical climbing, but never attacked anything as big as the Diamond.

"I've been on photo shoots for a number of different projects in the Rockies. One time we visited the commune called Drop City in southern Colorado. If you're interested in joining a commune, I can give you some contacts. I've shot pictures for stories about training army guys near Leadville to become ski troops for WWII, I've written about life in the Steam Caves at Glenwood Springs, sugar beet harvesting in northern Colorado and their crazy irrigation system, concerts at Red Rocks, and weddings in the Garden of the Gods. I've got a lot of stories I could tell. But I doubt that is what you are really after.

"Come on, let me know what you are really up to. What is your real agenda here?"

Andrew sat back in his chair and decided, what the heck. He had nothing to lose by telling Farley about the Uncle Arvid treasure legend.

"OK, here's the deal. I have to decide what to do now that TT&T is closing. I don't want to just find a replacement job doing what I've been doing. I need a change – a challenge.

"I visited my Aunt Annie recently, and she told me a crazy story about a distant Uncle Arvid who went off to Colorado in the late 1800's. He sent an old tin box to his brother and claimed it held a secret that was going to make them all rich. Then he was never heard from again. Aunt Annie thinks I should go looking for Uncle Arvid's treasure. I am pretty sure that there's nothing to be found, but tramping around the Colorado mountains might be just the thing to get me out of this feeling that I don't have a clue about what next to do with my life.

"So, I guess what I'm really looking for is some advice about how I should equip myself for stomping around the mountains chasing wild geese. I've done a lot of hiking here in the northeast, but I suspect hiking on or off the trail in the Rocky Mountains is quite a bit different."

"Does the Uncle Arvid legend include a treasure map and clues?" Farley asked.

"Of course."

"Do you seriously expect to discover a treasure chest and retire wealthy?"

"No. But I hope to have a little fun looking."

"At least you're smart enough to know that chasing around the high country is considerably different from hiking up to High Point in New Jersey, or hiking the Appalachian Trail.

"OK, if you're serious about this you need to do some research; figure out where you're going and who you might be meeting. In the first place, you're going to appear to the locals as a crazy flat lander. You can't let folks know you are running around the mountains treasure hunting. There are actually a lot of real lost treasure stories, and more than a few folks who take them seriously. I think you need some kind of cover story. Hmm... Pretending to be a nature photographer might not be a bad idea. I can suggest some basic equipment for that."

Farley continued, "There are other things to learn about the mountains. For example, there is not a day in the high country when it might not snow. I have seen folks start out on a sunny day in Denver with clear blue skies and the temperature around 80, and then come back later when it is still 80, but at 12,000 feet on Trail Ridge road they got caught in a snowstorm. In Colorado, you should never start a trip to the mountains without your down filled parka along.

"If you are driving, never leave town without a full tank of gas. It's easy to be in places where you can be 100 miles or more from the nearest gas station.

"When hiking in the high country, don't forget to breathe. It sounds silly, but at ten or twelve thousand feet there's not much oxygen. Pilots are required to have oxygen if they fly over ten thousand feet, but you can easily get higher than that hiking in the high country. Flat landers can make themselves sick by not breathing enough.

"Also, it's easy to get into trouble hiking off trail in the mountains. You can be following a game trail, and all of a sudden miss a switchback and find yourself stuck where it's nearly impossible to proceed.

"The climate in the high country depends on elevation. A change of one thousand feet at the same latitude has about the same effect as going 500 miles north or south at the same elevation. The tree line in Colorado is around eleven thousand five hundred feet. At 12,000 feet you'll find plants similar to those found in the tundra of the far north.

"Unless you want to pack everything you own on your back, I suggest establishing a base somewhere. If you are going to be there for very long, you'll also need an address. How about money?"

"I don't think money is going to be a problem. We're receiving a very nice severance package from TT&T."

Farley nodded, "Well, you're not going to carry all of your money with you are you? You won't be able to use New Jersey checks in Colorado; credit cards work most places. Traveler's checks are useful, but not in small towns or local shops in the mountains.

"By the way, if you don't mind saying, where is the location of this legendary treasure anyway? It's not likely that I'm going to jump your claim."

Andrew replied, "It's located somewhere near a place called Lulu City, which seems to be a ghost town near Grand Lake."

"You might not believe this, Andrew, but some years back I did a freelance photo shoot for a naturalist who was studying elk. He wanted pictures of the elk herd he was studying on the west side of Rocky Mountain National Park. The elk were located near a place called Andrew's Peak and Andrew's Peak is not too far from Grand Lake. Maybe that's some sort of sign for you.

"Anyway, I made my base in a cabin at a place called Elk Park Ranch, just north of Grand Lake. They had a nice main lodge, several rental cabins, and are probably still in business since the ranch has been there for many years. That could be just your ticket."

"If you're serious about this, and like the fake photographer angle, at lunchtime in the next day or so, we could make a run to some pawn shops, and get you properly outfitted."

Andrew asked, "Why not go to a regular camera store and buy a new camera? I don't have a problem with the cost."

"Because that would be like going on a hike in the mountains wearing brand new unwashed jeans. You don't want to scream 'tenderfoot or faker' to the locals, do you?"

Fortunately, there was not much left to do at TT&T. The next several days were spent with Farley trying to teach Andrew photography fundamentals. They found a used Nikon F 35mm SLR (Single Lens Reflex) camera, added a 100 to 300mm zoom lens from Spiratone, and a beat up camera bag.

Farley explained that the diagonal measurement of a 35mm film image is close to 50mm and this was why a 50mm lens is considered 'normal.' A 100mm lens provided a 2X magnification and a 300mm lens was similar to looking through a 6 power telescope. The 100 to 300mm zoom range would allow zooming in on a distant subject. In the rocky mountain high country, the air was clean and bright, and you can spot things a lot further away than in the eastern hills. To capture big game animals on film required a telephoto lens.

As they were searching for a camera, Farley told an old story that illustrated how the clear high altitude mountain air made it hard for the average easterner to judge distances.

"The story goes" Farley related, "a flat lander from the east was visiting his rancher cousin out west. As they walked around the ranch he asked his cousin to guess how far it was to a stand of trees on a nearby hill.

"I'd say those little trees are a couple of hundred yards away."

The rancher replied, "Those are 60' foot tall ponderosa pine trees, and they're three miles away. See that big flat topped mesa over there? How far away do you think that is?"

"Well, from what you told me about the trees, I would say it must be 10 or 15 miles away."

"Nope, that there mesa is thirty miles away." replied the rancher. "Now, you see that snow capped peak? How far away do you think that is?"

"OK, I think I'm getting the idea here. I guess that it's probably at least 60 miles to there."

"That's Long's Peak. It's 95 miles from here."

They walked around the ranch for a while observing the grazing cattle, and once spotted a distant herd of antelope. Then it was time to head back to the ranch house.

"Come on now, let's jump across the irrigation ditch and take a shortcut back," The rancher said.

"Not me," said the easterner. "For all I know, that sucker is a mile wide." ☺

"The point is," said Farley, "don't be fooled by distances in the high country. They say when Zebulon Pike and his crew first spotted what is now known as 'Pike's Peak', he thought he could easily climb to the summit. Three days later his party had only made it to some foothills before the snow was too deep to go on."

Farley then got on with his photography lessons. There was the F-stop and shutter speed business. Film was available with different ASA ratings. ASA 100 was for normal work, while ASA 400 was more sensitive and better in low light or where faster shutter speeds were required.

Shutter speeds? Proper exposure of film required a certain amount of light to hit the film. The faster the shutter speed, the less light gets on the film, so a larger F-stop or aperture size was required. F8 was a smaller lens opening then F4, and let in less light so a longer exposure was required for F8. The smaller the aperture, the better the focus and depth of field, but the slower the shutter speed the more moving things get blurry. There's always a compromise between shutter speed and F-stop.

F-stop, shutter speed, depth of field, film speed...
Andrew's head started spinning and his eyes started to
glaze over. However, Andrew was a good student and
researcher. He later visited the library and found some
books on photography basics and did a quick read. He
also stopped by a newsstand and bought the latest issue
of Popular Photography magazine, read it cover to
cover, and studied the ads. After several days, he felt
he could at least use the basic language of
photographers in case he had to pass as a real
photographer.

———————————————☞———————————————

Getting so involved with photography, Andrew
suddenly realized he had subconsciously committed
himself to chasing Uncle Arvid's Colorado wild goose.
With that realization, he started doing some serious
research. He wanted to learn as much as he could
about life in Colorado at the time Arvid was there. The
papers in the old tin box mentioned Lulu City, so
Andrew headed to the library to see what he could find
about Lulu City.

In the history books, Lulu City was known as a
'flash in the pan.' It's largest population was never
much more than 500, and at one time it had a hotel, a
store, a couple of saloons and bawdy houses, and even

a post office. It was established in 1879 by a Mr. Burnett who named it after his daughter.

Burnett and his followers hoped mineral traces would lead to large deposits of silver, or even gold. For several years, prospectors and entrepreneurs made Lulu City a busy place. What little ore was found was too far from any mill, and transportation cost more than the value of the processed ore. A few flakes of gold were panned from the stream, which was actually the headwaters of the Colorado River, but no one ever struck it rich there. By 1889, Lulu City was a ghost town. Eventually the area was incorporated into the west side of Rocky Mountain National Park. By 1960, there were only a few logs from rotting cabins and a few stones marking graves in the Lulu City Cemetery.

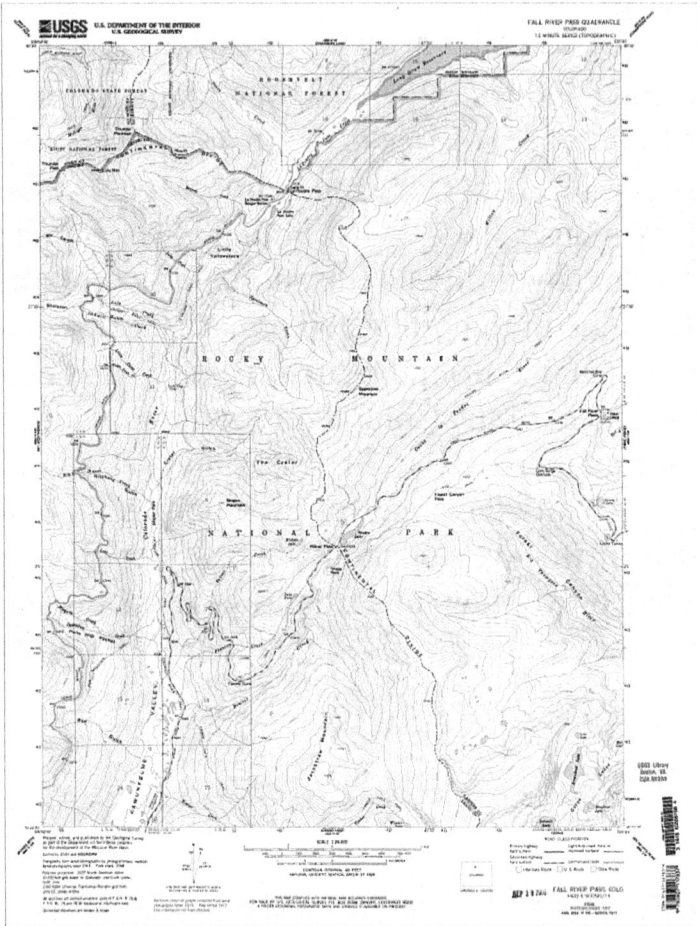

Andrew found a store in New York that
specialized in maps. He was able to buy a 7.5 minute
USGS topographical map that covered the area around
Lulu City. Back at his apartment, he spread the USGS

map out on the kitchen table. Then he dug out Uncle
Arvid's crude map.

He placed the maps side by side.

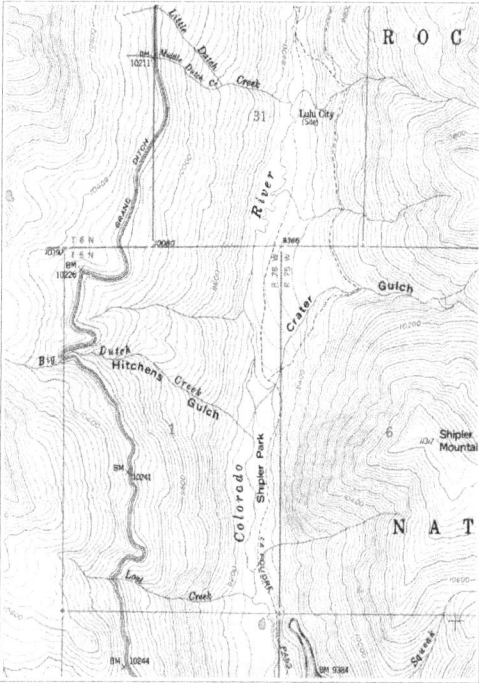

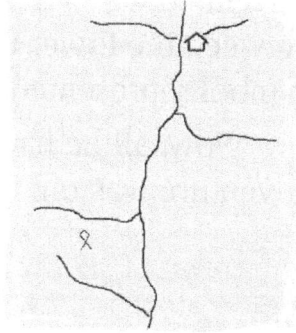

Arvid's map had several lines that looked like
streams, and there were also two symbols. One looked
like a crude house. Andrew decided the house symbol
represented Lulu City. The other symbol was more
difficult to decipher, but eventually Andrew discovered
an article on Viking era symbols. The symbol on the
map, Andrew decided, was a rune.

Andrew compared Arvid's map with the USGS map. The topographical map showed the location of Lulu City at the meeting point of two streams. Below Lulu City on the topographical map were three streams, one to the east and two to the west. These correlated with Arvid's map. The second symbol was between the lower two streams. Andrew guessed that symbol represented the location of Arvid's treasure.

Now, all he had to do was travel to Colorado. The adventure was on.

## Chapter 8 - Uncle Arvid's Travels.

Uncle Nils had translated *Arvid Jonssons underbara resa genom America* as *Arvid Jonsson's wonderful travels in America.* The collection of pages started in Sweden. Arvid described how, through various jobs, he had saved enough money to follow his brother to America. But, he vowed he would not follow Olof to what he considered a dreary life of hard work, lacking any fun and adventure.

Until he was 14, Arvid worked at the small family farm near Tvååker, Sweden. When the harvest was poor and there was not enough work to do, Arvid was loaned out to neighbor farms to help with horses and other livestock. At 14, he was apprenticed to a blacksmith. When the blacksmith shop lost business because of economic difficulties in Sweden, he was sent to work in a boatyard in Galtabäck. When he was 18, he decided to follow his brother Olof to America.

There were many Swedes on the ship to America. Most were poor families who had suffered several years of bad crops resulting in near poverty, and who dreamed of starting over in what was promised to be a land of plenty. Many of these folks had relatives or friends who had sent letters from America back to Sweden describing how even a poor family could get a large farm and prosper. The ocean trip took two months, and life for passengers was rough. Below decks it was crowded, smelly, and generally unpleasant. Steerage passengers usually were not allowed on deck, but Arvid with his experiences working at the Galtabäck boat yards, made himself useful to the crew and was able to escape the terrible conditions below deck.

Without an invitation, he jumped in and assisted crew members setting sails and even swabbing the deck from time to time. He was sort of adopted by a sailor from England who, during their free time, taught Arvid English. By the end of the trip, Arvid could understand some basic spoken English, and could make himself understood in simple conversations.

Other passengers, mostly the young bachelors on board, repeated stories they had heard of mountains full of gold in America, just waiting for an energetic Swede to pick the gold right out of the ground. There were also stories of dangerous Indians and wild bears and wolves. But, as is frequently the case, the young single men felt ready for any challenge. Arvid had had enough of groveling for demanding employers back in Sweden, dreamed of finding independence in America, and maybe his own riches. He was smart enough, however, to suspect that one had to do more than walk around waiting for gold to jump into his pockets. He was willing and ready to work for his treasure. Once he landed in New York, he started searching for a way to get to the fabled mountains of gold.

He arrived in America in the 1800's just at the time new railroads were pushing west. The transcontinental railroad had only recently been completed. The race to build the railroad resulted in many sections of inferior roadbed, and much work had to be done to improve the initial structures. Also, once the way was open to the west, a great migration followed. As a result, more and more sections of new railroads were required, and railroad jobs were pretty easy to get. The problem for Arvid was how to find a job that would lead to the gold mountains.

When people think of Swedes in America, most think of Minnesota. However, so many Swedes moved to Chicago that by the late 1800's several Swedish language newspapers were published there. A number of the passengers on Arvid's ship had relatives in Chicago and talked about job opportunities there. Arvid made friends with a couple of Chicago bound families and trailed along with them.

Just getting to the train station was a challenge. First, there was a ferry ride to New Jersey among a crush of people speaking many different languages, and carrying everything imaginable with them. Getting from the ferry terminal to the train station was difficult, but for a healthy young single man it was not so bad.

For poor families, carrying most of their important possessions and herding large groups of young children, it was very difficult. Arvid made himself useful with Swedish immigrants by helping with the luggage and keeping children from the large families in line. He became popular, and was soon treated as another family member. Not a few Swedish mothers looked at Arvid as a good match for their daughters. Arvid certainly liked the attention he received from young Swedish girls, but he remained focused on his main goal which did not include settling down quite yet.

The trip to Chicago was in itself an adventure for the Swedish travelers. Most were riding a train for the first time, and some worried whether people could actually survive the reported speeds of 35 miles per hour or more. Most of the time, however. the trains did not get close to the maximum speed. The train tracks were pretty rough, the seats were crude, and by the end of a day of travel, the passengers were more than a little worse for the wear. There was also danger along the way; in those days train wrecks were common.

The trip to Chicago took most of three days. Many stopping points had very crude facilities, or sometimes no facilities at all. When he arrived in Chicago, Arvid stuck with some Swedes who had relatives there. They found their way to an area called Swede Town. As a single man with some skills, Arvid found a number of job opportunities. Some, like jobs with the Pullman Company, were less than desirable. Although the company provided housing and stores for the workers, the pay scale was set so low people could barely survive. Eventually it got so bad there were bloody strikes.

Since Arvid wanted to continue on to the fabled west, he found work on a railroad crew repairing and upgrading tracks laid in haste during the race to construct the Transcontinental Railroad. Towns that sprung up at the end of each phase of construction of the

Transcontinental Railroad were known as 'Hell on Wheels.' Most of these were temporary collections of tents and shacks full of gambling dens and brothels designed to swallow the meager paychecks of the laborers. Although these towns didn't last long, there were still plenty of opportunities for the railroad workers to lose their money. Arvid was careful and managed to save enough for a grubstake.

At night in the labor camps, there was a lot of talk about guys who had struck it rich in the gold fields. There were arguments about whether it was better to head for proven places like Central City or Leadville, to search for your own mother load, or to go to a new place and get in early.

Arvid quit his railroad job when he got to Laramie, Wyoming. Following gossip and rumors about new ore strikes, he decided to head for Lulu City. He made his way from Laramie, Wyoming, to Ft. Collins, Colorado. There he picked up the basics for prospecting, including a bedroll, pick, shovel, and backpack. He then made his way up the Poudre River valley to the continental divide and followed the haul road down into the Colorado River valley to Lulu City.

By this time the population of Lulu City was a few hundred, and the rough buildings included a store and a couple of bars. Arvid hung around for a time just listening to conversations and learning about the mining business. He found a blacksmith shop and got a job helping the blacksmith fixing and forging tools, making nails, and keeping the forge fired up. In addition to making a few dollars, he was allowed to sleep in a corner of the shop at night.

Many of the Lulu City residents were recent immigrants and tended to stick together with people from their own homeland. There were only a few Scandinavians. One day a group of Germans got together for a party trip to Grand Lake. Upon returning to Lulu City, most of the group was drunk and created a major disturbance in the town. The next day the town leaders ordered the Germans to leave and never return. They ended up establishing a town up above Lulu City called Dutchtown.

Life in these mining boom towns was pretty rough. Whenever Arvid could get away from the forge, he wandered around in the nearby mountains, careful to avoid active claims. Claim jumping in those days was considered worse than horse stealing, and jumping a claim was a good way to make a short trip to the cemetery. Apparently this did not happened too often in Lulu City since there were only seven crude stones marking graves in the Lulu City cemetery.

By now Arvid had spent time observing how the mining business operated. A few smart business men managed to find investors to finance work on their claims. There were also many individual prospectors who worked hard and stayed broke. A little gold dust could be found in the Colorado River and small streams feeding it, but not enough gold dust to make it worth setting up a big dredging operation like those found in Breckenridge or South Park. There was, however, ore to be found in the area. By careful observation, Arvid learned how to recognize the kind of rocks that contained silver. On one of Arvid's hikes into the nearby mountains, he found a narrow hidden gulch that seemed to have the right kind of rock.

During Arvid's apprenticeship with a blacksmith back in Sweden, he was taught about the ancient methods the vikings used to make iron. He had also learned that the melting point for silver was lower than the melting point for iron. Arvid built a small bank furnace, fired it with dried ponderosa pine branches, loaded it with some silver ore, made a bellows to increase the temperature, and managed to create a small silver ingot.

Thrilled that he had a site with silver ore, he had to try and find a way to turn his discovery into a working mine. Turning silver ore into ingots would require a much bigger investment than he could make on his own. He needed financial help from outside. He decided to put together an investment group from successful east coast Swedish businessmen. Arvid made a map of his discovery which he bundled along with his silver ingot, and mailed the package to his brother back east for safe keeping until he could travel back to the east coast and try to organize a company.

Arvid left Lulu City and boarded a train for the long trip back east. Somewhere around Jamesville, Iowa, a flash flood had damaged a bridge across Sevenmile Creek. The train's engine broke through the bridge, the passenger cars collapsed into a mangled mess, and Arvid and his dreams died in the wreck.

# Arvid's Treasure

## Chapter 9 - The Adventure Train

Andrew had spent several weeks researching and preparing for his trip to Colorado. Per recommendations from Farley, he made contact with the manager of Elk Park Ranch, made a reservation and paid in advance for a cabin for two months, with an option to extend his stay. Andrew then shipped several boxes to the ranch to be held there until his arrival.

Andrew also created credit and debit card accounts and deposits with Bank America. This would allow him to withdraw cash from banks anywhere in the country. He also set up electronic funds transfer so he could easily move money from his mutual funds to his bank accounts. This, he hoped, would eliminate any problems with companies that did not accept out-of-state bank checks.

He arranged to store a few items like his bike and a few small household goods in Aunt Annie's garage. On his last visit with Aunt Annie, she said she would miss him, but approved his plan.

Andrew went to Pennsylvania Station and bought a 15 day rail pass that allowed him to get on and off trains up to 8 times within the 15 days. Shouldering his backpack, he started his journey west. The train ride from New York City to Chicago took most of two days. Andrew had not purchased a ticket for a sleeper car, since he wanted to see as much of the country as possible; there was indeed a lot of lovely landscape along the way. The train tracks also went through a lot of dilapidated and ugly industrial areas. There were occasional long waits while the train paused to let freight trains go by. Much of the trip was after dark when the scenery was next to invisible. Arvid decided that if he ever made the trip again, he would opt for a sleeping car.

The stop in Chicago required changing trains and killing a couple of hours between trains. He wandered around the station a bit, grabbed a snack, and picked up a couple of books. His experience so far had taught him that gazing at the landscape and scenery was not a full time activity on a long train ride.

As he made his way to the crowded train platform for the next part of his trip, he was blind sided by a woman who was fighting to drag her apparently overloaded large red suitcase over a curb. As she was pulling the big suitcase, it stuck. She gave it a hard tug that suddenly released the suitcase. Her spike heel slipped on the pavement and sent her flying into Andrew who grabbed her to keep her from falling. If Andrew had not been in the path of the collision, she would probably have flown herself and her baggage clear across the platform. He automatically said, "Excuse me, miss," even though she crashed into him rather the other way around.

The girl was dressed in clothes that looked like they came right out of a Frederick's of Hollywood bargain bin. She was wearing spike heels, a mini skirt, and a frilly blouse that in Andrew's opinion were very impractical for chasing trains.

"Oh well," Andrew thought, "I've seen stranger dress choices on the New York City streets, but the coeds on the Fairleigh Dickinson University campus have better sense." Andrew boarded the train, chose a seat, and settled in for the next part of his train ride adventure

Not long into the ride, Andrew made his way to the toilet near the end of the train car. The small sign on the door indicated 'vacant' so he opened the door to enter and simultaneously heard a shriek, a female voice shout 'pervert' and caught a glimpse of a naked girl apparently in the midst of changing clothes. He quickly closed the door except for a small gap and said through the gap "sorry, but the sign on the door said vacant. If you don't want any more unwanted visitors, you better lock the door." He then closed the door and returned to his seat until a toilet was free.

Later, after making a trip to the toilet, he noticed a woman rearranging things in a big red suitcase. He took a seat across the aisle from her and jokingly remarked, "I'm not really a member of the PCA, but you might be a member of the FESA."

She looked up from arranging things in the suitcase and said, "What are you talking about? What on earth is the PCA, and what is the FESA?"

"PCA is the Perverts Club of America. You accused me of being a member when you forgot to lock the toilet door and tricked me into opening it. That makes you a possible member of the FESA, the Female Exhibitionist Club of America."

"Oh!… I'm sorry for shrieking at you, but I'm not used to people barging in on me like that."

"Well, if I was a dedicated member of the PCA, I would have kept the door open a lot longer. After I closed it, I kind of wished I was a PCA member, because what little I saw was very attractive, he grinned.

"I see you decided to change out of those silly spike heels before you stumble and push some other guy around on the train platform."

Jane looked more closely at Andrew, "Oh...was that you I crashed into? I should've thanked you for saving me, but I was so embarrassed I just wanted to get out of there as fast as possible. I never wear spike heels, and they are terrible for walking, and I felt stupid for wearing them."

"You can't say you never wear spike heels, because if I was called as a witness I would swear under oath that I saw you wearing them. At least it looks like you changed into more sensible traveling clothes."

"I don't dress like that. I mean that it is not how I usually dress. I was visiting an old college friend of mine who's studying fashion design at Northwestern University. She insisted in dressing me in what she considers the latest fashion. I just couldn't bring myself to hurt her feelings by refusing to let her 'improve' my appearance. She thought my normal cowgirl outfit needed to be improved."

"Well, in my opinion, if what you're wearing now is what you call your cowgirl outfit it's a big improvement over what the woman I saw on the train platform was wearing. I better not say what my impression of you was as you were stumbling and wobbling on your way to the train. Of course, if I actually was a dedicated member of PCA, I might think differently. Are you a college student like your friend?"

"Sort of post college actually. I have a Master's degree in Wildlife Management from Colorado State. I was visiting my former roommate who is now studying fashion design at Northwestern. In our undergraduate days we were pretty close, but I'm afraid I discovered that sometimes friends move on in different directions. What about you? Where are you from and where are you heading?"

"I've lived most of my life in New Jersey. For the last several years I've been commuting to work in New York City; but my company recently went out of business, so I'm taking some time to, as they say, try to discover myself."

Jane was interested, "What were you doing in New York?"

"I was working for TT&T, that is *Tales, Trails and Tails* magazine. Their circulation numbers were down and the owner, who's close to retirement, decided to give it up."

"So your current job title is 'unemployed'?"

"Yes, but that's not as bad as it sounds. The TT&T owner is a very generous guy, and he provided his employees with a very nice severance package that'll keep me going for a while."

"So what are your plans? I'm sorry, this is really none of my business. I'm not usually such a nosy person."

Andrew smiled, "That's OK. I've done a lot of traveling on commuter trains and it's interesting how sometimes it's easy to talk about personal things to a complete stranger. You sit next to someone on a commuter train to New York, and before you get to Seacaucus you know all about their family feuds, boring wife, children's health problems, or whatever. I'm no longer surprised at how strangers on a train share personal things, and I can sometimes tell complete strangers things I don't share with my closest friends."

Andrew paused for a moment, "I have an Aunt Annie who is of the opinion that I have never gotten past being an overgrown college student. I've been living in the same apartment I moved into as a student at Fairleigh Dickinson University. It's been easy to commute from there to the TT&T offices in New York, so why move? Aunt Annie keeps pushing me to get out of my shell and explore the world.

"Maybe she's right. Maybe I haven't quite gotten past being an overgrown college student. Anyway, here I am, taking my first trip to Colorado, facing the great unknown... maybe I'm just trying to find myself."

Jane asked, "What do your parents think about all of this?"

"Nothing. My parents were killed in an automobile accident when I was a freshman in college. Aunt Annie doesn't have any children of her own and has made it her business to keep my life focused."

"I'm sorry about your parents. Here I go, being rude and nosy again."

"No problem. What about you? You said you were a 'post student.' What does that mean? Are you in graduate school, or what?"

"I'm thinking of going back to graduate school, but unless I can get some kind of research grant, financing is an issue. My parents would probably help, but their lives are pretty complicated and I don't want to have to beg for money from them."

"What do you mean by complicated? Uh oh! Now I'm being the nosy one."

"That's OK. My dad's parents have a ranch that's been in the family for generations. When my dad and mom got married, they moved to the ranch. My grandparents assumed that my dad would eventually take over the ranch, but my dad had other ideas. My mom was more of a city girl and never accepted the idea of being a rancher's wife. With so much friction in the family, when I was 10 years old my parents moved to Denver.

"Eventually, my dad shocked everyone by moving in with his boyfriend. My mom had a few boyfriends of her own. Since I became an inconvenience for them, I was shipped back to the ranch and was basically raised by my grandparents. That was the best thing that could've happened to me, since I love the ranch.

"These days I have a job at another ranch on the Colorado west slope. It's not quite a dude ranch, but they have some cabins and a lot of summer guests. I help with the horses, clean the barns and the guest rooms, and the swimming pool, do miscellaneous chores, and occasionally lead nature hikes for tourists."

"It sounds like there's no husband or significant other in the picture."

"Nope! I've had a few boyfriends, but nothing really very serious. What about you? Have you left a string of broken hearts along the way?"

"I did have a girl friend in college. After we graduated, she preferred the big city, and got a job in New York. She pushed on me, wanting to get an apartment together, but I told her that I felt claustrophobic in big cities. That was the deal breaker.

"Do you think you've found your place in life at your Colorado mountain ranch?"

"Not really. I would like to stay in Wildlife Management, but the jobs are few and far between."

Jane continued, "I have an Uncle Bill, sort of like your Aunt Annie. Uncle Bill works for the Colorado Parks and Wildlife Headquarters Office in Fort Collins. He's been my mentor through my college days, and might be able to find some part time contract work for me that would keep me closer to my major and help fund some post graduate studies. One of my university research projects was studying grass shrimp in Sheep Lakes in Rocky Mountain National Park. I'm hoping that some day I might be able to get on with the National Park Service."

The train started to slow down, and an announcement came over the PA system. "Because of problems up the line, we will be making an unscheduled stop at Jamesville, Iowa."

A conductor came hurrying through the car and Andrew stopped him and asked what was going on.

"There was a flash flood at Sevenmile Creek that weakened the bridge, and an east bound freight crashed and destroyed a large section of the track. This train isn't going anywhere any time soon. Since you don't have a ticket for a sleeper, if I were you, I'd find a place in town to hole up for a couple of days."

As the train slowly pulled into Jamesville, Andrew looked through the window and spied a motel sign that said 'Wigwam Motel'.

"There's a motel over there. Maybe we could get a room. How about it, Jane? Let's make a run for it."

"I think I'd rather stay on the train." Jane replied uncertainly, thinking about her empty wallet.

The voice on the PA system announced, "All coach passengers must disembark at this stop."

Andrew threw his backpack over his shoulder, grabbed Jane's suitcase and said, "Oh, come on! You can't spend a couple days on an empty train."

---

Jane had no option but to chase after him. They hurried up the street toward the motel sign, entered the Wigwam Motel reception area, and Andrew put the Jane's suitcase down near the reception desk.

Meanwhile, Jane asked the receptionist if there was a phone she could use. The receptionist told her she could use the phone on the table by the front door. Jane had a problem. Her visit to Janice had cost more than she expected, and she didn't have enough money left to cover expenses for this unplanned stop. Jane tried to place a collect call to her Uncle Bill, but there was no answer.

Andrew asked the receptionist, who Andrew decided resembled Aunt Annie's next door neighbor Martha, about the availability of rooms.

"We only have one room left. I'm sorry, it's our most expensive room, but I think you and your wife would probably be very comfortable there."

She gave Andrew a knowing smile, and he thought he detected a sly wink. Andrew was surprised that she assumed Jane was his wife. Since they had come in together and he had carried her suitcase, it was probably a natural assumption on her part. He was about to correct her, but then realized he had two choices. He could insist that he and Jane were not a couple, but that would mean that one of them would have no place to stay. The conductor had said the train might be stuck in town for several days. With no time for second thoughts, Andrew said, "We'll take it," handed over his credit card, and wrote Mr. and Mrs Olofsson on the registration form.

The receptionist handed Andrew two room keys, and said "Here are your keys, go down the hall to the right, room 106." And with another wink she added, "I'm sure you and your wife will love the room."

Andrew found Jane sitting on a bench at the phone table, sat down next to her, waiting for her to finish her call. She looked disturbed as she hung up and dialed another number. Again there seemed to be no answer.

She put down the phone, shook her head in exasperation and confided, "I have a problem. I spent nearly all my cash visiting Janice. I have some money in my checking account, but no one's going to accept an out-of-state check. I tried calling Uncle Bill in hopes he could wire me enough money to get back to Colorado, but there's no answer."

"Worry not!" Andrew smiled sheepishly, "We just got married, and so now my money is your money."

"What do you mean just got married? What are you talking about?"

Andrew explained the situation.

"Aunt Martha assumed that we were together."

"Aunt Martha?"

"The receptionist is a nice lady who reminds me of Martha, Aunt Annie's next door neighbor. Anyway, she claimed there was only one room available here, or even in the whole town, but was sure my wife and I would like the room. How could I argue with such a sweet old lady? If I had told her we were not together, either you or I would be out in the cold for as long as the train is stuck here. I certainly don't want to sleep on a park bench, and I would hate myself if I caused you to have to find a bench or cardboard box or whatever. So, I decided to let the nice lady continue to believe we were a couple, and took the room. We can work something out. If necessary, I'll sleep in the bathtub.

"Here's your room key, She gave us two."

Jane wasn't sure about the arrangement, "This is crazy! I can't pay for even half of a motel room. And I don't like the idea of sharing a room with a complete stranger."

"First of all, we're not complete strangers. I've probably already told you more about myself than I've ever told any girl I've dated. Secondly, I've already seen you naked. So you don't have to worry about that. Third, don't worry about the cost, I've got us covered.

"How about this? You can be Claudette Colbert and I can be Clark Gable in 'It happened One Night.' We can always hang a blanket across the room."

"But... Wait a minute... who are Claudette Colbert and Clark Gable?"

"I can't believe you've never seen 'It Happened One Night.' It's a major movie classic. Come on, let's not make Aunt Martha think we're having a spat."

Jane mused, "Well, I guess I don't have much choice do I? You might not be a member of the PCA, but I just hope you are not Andrew the Ripper."

"Trust me. If you are too worried, you can tie my hands and blindfold me while you're changing."

Andrew picked up her suitcase and his backpack and headed to their room with Jane nervously following. They checked room numbers on the doors as they went down the hall until they found room 106.

"Why is our room number on a large red heart?" Jane asked suspiciously.

"I'm not sure. It looks like dear old 'Aunt Martha' put us in the Honeymoon Suite." She did say it was the only room left."

Andrew opened the door and stepped aside to let Jane enter while he reached for her suitcase.

The room was indeed a Honeymoon Suite; red walls, a picture with cute flying cupids over a king sized bed covered with a plush red cover and a pile of heart shaped pillows greeted them.

"This is too much. I'll have nightmares trying to sleep here." Jane exclaimed.

"Don't worry, your eyes will be closed when you're asleep, and you won't see a thing."

"Oh! There's even a heart shaped Jacuzzi tub over there!"

"Well, I guess we'll just have to rough it. Look at this big basket of fruit, cheese, and crackers. What do you suppose is in the mini bar? Yep, a nice bottle of champagne with a tag 'complements of the house'. No wonder it's the most expensive room in the place. Wow! That's a big TV and it's complete with a VTR and a collection of tapes. This is living! Look!"

Jane was wary, "I told you I can't afford this. Oh! There are even soft fuzzy pink and blue robes here in the bathroom, and a shower big enough for two or more. And the towels are also pink and blue."

"OK, Let's take turns in the bathroom, and then find something to eat."

While Jane took her turn, Andrew checked out the room info book and found instructions for operating the hot tub. The first step was to fill the tub. The instructions noted that when the start switch was pressed, the tub would automatically fill to the proper level and heat the water.

"What have you done to the hot tub?" Jane asked when she came out of the bathroom. "It's filling and bubbling."

"I thought that every girl's dream was a nice soak in a whirlpool bath."

"You don't think I'm going to get in that thing with you in the room, do you?"

"Just remember. You can always invoke the tied hands and blindfold clause in our agreement. Let's see if Aunt Martha can recommend a good place for dinner."

Martha suggested Leone's, an Italian restaurant a couple of blocks away. It was clearly a popular place where everyone seemed to know everyone. They found a seat, and a waitress, wearing a blouse with the monogrammed name Francesca, came over, "I'll bet you folks came on the train. Did Martha send you?"

"That's right." Andrew replied. "Why do you think Martha sent us?"

"Because if you got off the train, the only place to stay is the Wigwam, and Martha is the restaurant owner's cousin. The scuttlebutt is the wreck at Sevenmile Creek won't be cleared up for a couple of days."

Andrew frowned, "That's not good news. I'm sure this is a very nice town, but we had hoped to be well on our way to Colorado by now. Oh well, what do you recommend for dinner."

"Most folks go with the spaghetti dinner special. Can't go wrong with that."

"Do you serve wine here?"

"Of course! One of the owner's cousins ships us several cases of Primitivo from Italy every couple of months. It's the real thing."

"Jane, could you live with a nice bottle of Primitivo along with the spaghetti dinner?"

"Uh… OK. I guess that sounds good. And could I also get a glass of water please."

"Coming right up."

Jane whispered to Andrew, "I told you I don't have any money, and you're unemployed. Are you sure you want to do this? Or will we end up as dishwashers?"

Andrew grinned, "Don't worry. My credit card account is still full from the severance package from TT&T. And don't forget, since Aunt Martha married us, my money is your money. Can you believe that just a couple of weeks ago I was eating at Leone's?"

Jane looked puzzled, "You mean you've been here before:"

"No, I mean Mama Leone's in New York City. I had dinner there with Farley, a fellow refugee from TT&T. He's partly responsible for my decision to go to Colorado.'

Francesca delivered wine glasses, poured some wine for them, and left the bottle.

"How did he convince you to go to Colorado?"

"Well, Aunt Annie had already put a bug in my ear. She told me a wild story about an Uncle Arvid, who traveled to Colorado in the late 1800's. He'd sent back a package with a note that claimed he was going to make the family rich."

"You mean he left some kind of treasure map?"

"I guess you might call it that. However, after the package arrived, the family never heard from him again. Anyway, Aunt Annie pushed me to follow the trail Uncle Arvid left. At first it seemed like a crazy idea. Then I decided that with the severance package from TT&T, I could afford to bum around for a while. I just couldn't bring myself to face the prospect of applying for a new job. I knew my friend Farley had spent time in Colorado, so I invited him to dinner, and he told some stories and descriptions of the mountains that made it sound exciting. So, I'm on my way."

"You mean you're chasing Uncle Arvid's legend?"

"I guess so. I don't really expect to find anything, but I guess it makes a good excuse to travel and get out of the rut Aunt Annie claims I've been in."

Francesca arrived with two heaping plates of spaghetti along with a large salad bowl, two salad plates, a basket of garlic bread, and a small dish of grated cheese.

"This is the house dressing, Italian, but I can get something else if you prefer."

"Italian is fine with me, what about you, Jane?"

"Italian seems appropriate here, Thanks, Francesca, There's no way I can finish this. I'm going to feel like a pig by the time we are through. Andrew, you were telling me about an Uncle Arvid."

"Yes. An old family legend claims when Arvid arrived from Sweden, he had dreams of striking it rich in America. He apparently worked his way west, and eventually sent a package back to the family in New Jersey. It contained a small silver ingot and a note that suggested he was going to make the family rich. The story ends there; he was never heard from again."

"And now you're going to try to discover Uncle Arvid's treasure, aren't you?"

"I doubt I'll find any treasure. But I expect to have a little fun looking."

Andrew and Jane continued sharing experiences as they ate the excellent spaghetti dinner special. Francesca came by a couple of times to see if they needed anything. They each ordered Zuppa Inglese for dessert, and Andrew said he doubted they could have had anything better at Mama Leone's in New York City. They lingered over the meal as long as possible;

neither could decide how they wanted the room sharing experience to play out.

Andrew kept refilling their wine glasses until the bottle was empty. He finally asked Francesca about the check, and she told them to pay on their way out.

On the wall near the cash register were several pictures of an old train wreck. Andrew asked Francesca about the pictures.

"Back in the 1800's a train wrecked going over Sevenmile Creek. It was close to the same place where the freight train crashed yesterday. That train was an eastbound passenger train, and a lot of people were killed. If you're interested, the Pioneer Museum, originally an old school house here in town, has a nice display about the wreck.

As they left Leone's, the sky was dark and they were attacked by a hard wind driven rainstorm. By the time they got to the Wigwam, they were completely soaked. They were quiet as they entered room 106. Andrew said, "I'm grateful for those fuzzy robes. Throw me one, and you can change in the bathroom."

Jane and Andrew changed into robes and hung their wet clothes on the shower rod. Andrew checked the hot tub which was now filled with bubbling hot water.

"Well, princess, it looks like your fancy bath awaits you."

"Forget it! There's no way I'm getting into that thing."

"Come on, every girl dreams about a nice soak in a bubbly hot tub. How many times have you had a chance like this? What are the chances you will ever see such a tub again? If you are afraid of me, you can always enforce the 'tie my hands and blindfold me' clause. We can dim the lights so you won't worry about whether I've decided to join the PCA."

Andrew turned off the overhead room light so that there was only a dim glow of light from the partially closed bathroom door. Jane went over to the hot tub and swirled the water with her hand. She decided Andrew seemed nice enough and wasn't too much of a threat. Or maybe he was a threat, and that thought provoked a strange slightly tingly feeling.

"How about just the blindfold?" She said with a low husky voice.

"OK. I promise I won't make rude comments, or play tickle and grab… unless you start it."

As Jane dug into her suitcase and found a scarf, Andrew dropped his robe and slipped into the tub. Jane came up behind him and carefully tied the scarf as a blindfold. Then Jane dropped her robe and slipped carefully under the bubbling tub water. The jets of warm water were soothing, and Jane fought the urge to close her eyes and doze off. Suddenly Jane felt something gently tickling her foot. She shook her head awake and said, "Are you playing footsie with me?"

"We've been in here for a long time now, and I'm starting to feel like a prune. You didn't answer my questions and seemed to be off in never never land."

Jane got out of the tub, put on the pink fuzzy robe, and then removed Andrew's blindfold and disappeared into the bathroom. Andrew climbed out of the tub, and put on the blue robe. Once they were both properly toweled and robed, Andrew suggested they watch something from the video collection, "What do you want to watch? There's a pretty large collection here. It seems to be a combination of soft porn and classics. Let's see, we've got 'Bathing Beauties of 1940,' 'What Modern Women Love,' 'Barefoot in the Park,' 'Debbie in Paris,' 'Irma la Douce,' 'Send Me No Flowers,' and...you are not going to believe this."

"What did you find?"

"They actually have a copy of 'It Happened One Night', "

"I'm guessing you consider it required viewing for me. Do you want something from the mini bar?"

"How about we open that complimentary bottle of champagne? Too bad we don't have any popcorn."

"I think I've had too much to drink already. The fruit basket also has cheese, crackers, and a nice box of chocolates."

The king sized bed was wide enough for them to build a wall of heart shaped pillows between them. They settled back, and watched the movie.

"I don't think we can stretch a blanket between us like Colbert and Gable, but the pillows should work." said Jane.

"Well, this bed is wide enough for us to avoid any unwanted entanglements. Good night, Colbert."

"Good night, Gable."

---

The next morning they agreed to see if Leone's was open for breakfast. Martha said it was, and recommended the Swedish pancakes.

"Swedish pancakes in an Italian restaurant?" asked Andrew.

"In the old days, this area had quite a few Swedish immigrants. And you'll probably find more Swedish than Italian influence in the culture of the area."

After stuffing themselves with pancakes, they got directions to the Pioneer Museum where they watched a video that described the building of the transcontinental railroad. The railroad was actually responsible for creating Jamesville. It was one of the few 'hell on wheels' communities remaining after the track construction moved on. It turned out the builders were in such a hurry to build the railroad, they did not take into account the poor unstable soil conditions in the Sevenmile Creek area. From the very beginning, the unstable ground was the cause of many train derailments.

A large section of the Museum was dedicated to 'The Great Jamesville Train Wreck.' The exhibit also included a lot of pictures and descriptions of the wreck. The photos made it clear that train wrecks can be terrible. Dozens of people died in the 1881 wreck at Sevenmile Creek.

Jane was reading an old newspaper article that told of a man found alive in the wreckage two days after the crash. She grabbed Andrew's sleeve, "Look at this, Andrew, you're not going to believe it!"

### Jamesville Star
### Monday March 13, 1881
### Man Rescued After Two Days in Wreckage

While clearing up the wreckage from the recent train wreck, the workers heard a faint voice crying for help. A man, with multiple injuries, was discovered under one of the wrecked passenger cars. The workers asked him who he was. He was barely able to speak, and spoke only in Swedish. Before he passed out, he said his name was Arvid Jonsson from Smalland, Sweden.

He was taken to the nearby farm of Oskar Larsson where the Larsson twins, Ida and Ada, are caring for him.

### Jamesville Star
### Thursday, March 16, 1881
### Train Wreck Victim Dies

The man pulled from the train wreck has died. He had been cared for by Ida and Ada Larsson. There will be a funeral service at the Swedish Lutheran Church on Saturday at 2 PM.

Andrew read from the clippings where Jane was pointing, "You're right! I can't believe this! That must be Aunt Annie's Uncle Arvid. I guess the mystery of what happened to Arvid is solved.

"At least he apparently was taken in and cared for by the Swedish community here. I would like to imagine he spent his last days being cared for by a couple of beautiful Swedish girls."

"It mentions the funeral service. Do you suppose we could find his grave?"

"It's worth a try. Maybe I could take a picture of it to send to Aunt Annie."

They talked to a volunteer at the museum reception desk and found out there was a cemetery beside the Lutheran Church several blocks north on the edge of town.

Finding the cemetery, they discovered an elderly couple tending flowers placed at the grave sites. When asked if they knew anything about a Swedish victim of the famous train wreck, they said that his grave was in the Larsson family plot. Andrew took several pictures to send to Aunt Annie.

Arvid Olofsson

victim of the
Jamesvill
Train Wreck

Walking back through town, they stopped at a grocery store and picked up a couple deli sandwiches and drinks. They found a picnic table in a small park next to the library, had a leisurely lunch, and then spent the rest of the day at the library.

Andrew found a book on the building of the transcontinental railroad and was surprised to learn how much Abraham Lincoln had been involved with railroad investments, and how he was in part responsible for government backing of the project. To help private companies fund construction, companies were given every other section of land for several miles on either side of the projected railroad line. Andrew discovered that the highest point on the line was just north of the Colorado border, about 50 miles as the crow flies from Lulu City.

After a leisurely afternoon at the library, they returned to Leone's for dinner. Francesca remembered them and suggested the daily special. They agreed. Joseph, the owner, came out and greeted them, "Ah! We are honored again to have the Honeymoon Couple with us."

Andrew protested, "We're not a honeymoon couple."

"But my cousin Martha tells me you are staying in the honeymoon suite. Anyone who stays in the honeymoon suite always receives complimentary wine at Leone's."

"But it was the only room available. We're not on a honeymoon."

"It matters not." Joseph happily proclaimed, "For you we have the special house wines, Francesca, bring a bottle of the special red Primitivo."

As they ate their way through the salad and pasta, Francesca frequently came by and refilled their glasses. By dessert, the bottle was nearly empty. Joseph reappeared, this time with a bottle of red Zinfandel.

"My cousin in Italy sends this to me. You must tell me which you like better, the Primitivo or the Zinfandel."

Andrew and Jane drank some Zinfandel while Joseph sat down near them and poured himself a glass of wine.

"What do your think? Eh! Please, a toast to my cousin who sends the wine."

They sipped. Joseph was clearly in a happy mood.

"A toast to Francesca, our best waitress, who is also a cousin of mine."

They all sipped again. Joseph refilled the glasses.

"Now a toast to the honeymooners."

In spite of their protests, Joseph's toasts continued until the bottle was empty.

As Andrew and Jane left Leone's and started back to the Wigwam Motel, Jane stumbled, and Andrew grabbed her arm to prevent her from falling. Jane mumbled, "I feel almost like I'm wearing Janice's spike heels."

"I think you're feeling the effects of the wine. You better hold my arm."

Jane protested, "You think I'm drunk? I only had a couple of glasses of wine."

"By the time Joseph was finished with his toasts, you had more than a couple of glasses. Did you know the wine we were drinking has more than four times the amount of alcohol of most American beer?"

"No, but I'm not a drinker. At Janice's party in Chicago, I refused to join in the drinking games. Janice said I was too uptight."

As they got closer to the Wigwam, Jane continued, "Janice called me old fashioned, and not liberated, and she even said I was a prude."

Andrew tried to console her, "You are a perfectly normal red-blooded girl. You shouldn't let those Chicago party people tell you how to behave. Let's just get you back to the room so you can let all that wine stop working on you."

As they returned to room 106, Andrew and Jane were feeling more relaxed together, and there was none of the tension they felt the night before. Jane went into the bathroom, undressed, and put on the pink bathrobe. Andrew changed into his blue bathrobe, and then turned on the Jacuzzi tub jets.

As Andrew enter the hot tub, Jane came out of the bathroom, found the blindfold, and remembering the criticisms Janice had thrown at her after the Chicago party, said to herself "To hell with you, Janice. I'm not a prude!" Jane tossed the blindfold away and slurred, "Andrew, do you think I'm a prude?"

She then slowly dropped her robe, posed for a minute, and then slid into the tub.

"I… I uh don't know what to say." Andrew mumbled, "Clearly you're not a prude… no… I uh… I… I think you're a little under the influence of the wine, but you are very beautiful. It might be awhile before I recover."

Jane felt a kind of warm tingly feeling as the hot tub bubbles surrounded her. As the effects of the wine diminished she thought, "What have I done. I can't believe I just did that."

After soaking quietly for a while, they got into their robes, picked out a video, lined up some snacks, and laid in bed watching the movie. Most of the tension was gone, but neither was sure what to make of the strange and somewhat intimate relationship that had developed.

The next morning the phone rang. 'Aunt Martha' at the desk informed them that the repairs to the train track went faster than expected, and they needed to get back to the train by noon if they wanted to continue their trip. They hurried through their morning routine, did some quick packing, and managed to gulp down some pancakes at Leone's before boarding the west bound train.

Maintaining a comfortable silence, each was lost in thoughts about the last couple of days, mentally reliving the details of their time together. Jane wondered, was I too impulsive? Should I have not agreed to share the room? Did I really drink that much wine?

Andrew also silently reviewed the experience. Did I say the right things? Should I have reacted differently? If I had to do it all again, how would I behave. Should I have just grabbed her and kissed her? Should I have reached out and pulled her closer when I had the chance?

Unanswered questions that were too late to answer. As the train rolled west, they fell back into the roles of 'strangers on a train'.

As the train approached Omaha, Nebraska, Andrew said, "I'm afraid this is where I get off. I'm switching trains and heading for Denver. I thought you were also going to Colorado."

"I am, but I'm headed for Ft. Collins; I'll stay on this train until Laramie and go to Ft. Collins from there."

The train slowed as it reached Omaha and Andrew picked up his backpack, "I guess this where we say goodbye. This has been a very unusual and delightful experience. Thank you for being a most excellent 'stranger on a train."

"It's been fun for me too. Can't you give me your address so that I can repay you for my share of the motel and meals?"

"Even though our 'Aunt Martha marriage' didn't last very long, you should assume we had a joint bank account for the duration, and you don't owe me a thing. Since I'm currently just wandering around 'looking for myself.' I don't really have a permanent address to give you anyway. Maybe we'll cross paths again someday."

"Not very likely, but thank you again."

Andrew shouldered his backpack, and left the train. Jane watched him walk across the platform as the train moved on.

Arvid's Treasure

## Chapter 10 - Jane Accepts A Challenge

Jane left the train in Laramie, Wyoming. She still had the problem of having very little money in her pocket. She noticed some girls who looked like coeds; one of them was hugging another, who had just gotten off the train. Approaching them, Jane asked if they were going to the University of Wyoming campus, and if she could bum a ride to the Wyoming Union building. Having visited the UW campus a number of times when she was a student at Colorado State, she knew her way around. In the Union building, she located the ride board, and found someone who was going to Ft. Collins, Colorado. Her ride dropped her off at the Lory Student Center at Colorado State University. She found a phone, called to see if her Uncle Bill was available, and walked to Uncle Bill's Colorado Parks and Wildlife Headquarters office.

Uncle Bill gave her a hug, and she told him a little about her Chicago adventure, leaving out her train ride experience. Bill listened to her account of how Janice seemed to have become a different person since their roommate days. Bill agreed that some friendships do not stand the test of time because people can change their interests and beliefs.

"Are you headed back to your Grand Lake job?" Bill asked.

"Yes, at least for the rest of the summer. I'm trying to save enough money to be able to return to CSU for some post graduate courses; maybe something that might make me eligible to apply for a National Park job."

"I don't know of any open scholarship or grant programs right now, but I'll keep my feelers out." Bill thought for a moment, "I'm working on a case involving some serious poaching. There's been a number of incidents where poachers have killed trophy elk, big horn sheep, and mule deer, taken the heads, and left the bodies to rot. There's a profitable market for these trophy heads. I guess some rich folks are willing to pay a lot of money for a trophy, but don't want to bother going through the rigors of a real hunt; or for that matter, could care less about legal hunting seasons. There are rumors that a Texan recently paid over $20,000 for a trophy elk head."

"Where's this poaching going on?"

"You know the Poudre River headwaters area? There are jurisdictional issues up there. You have Rocky Mountain National Park, Arapaho and Roosevelt National Forest, and Jackson, Larimer, and Grand Counties, all coming together in the high country of the Poudre and Colorado River headwaters. When a poaching incident occurs, it's sometimes not clear what agency is responsible for following up on the report.

"This area is bigger than some eastern states, and enforcement officers are spread very thin. This jurisdictional problem, together with the fact that this area contains a concentration of trophy elk, big horn sheep, and mule deer, makes it a target for the trophy poachers. Since there's no hunting in the National Park, more trophy animals develop, and poachers are tempted to take advantage of the situation."

"What can I do?" Jane asked.

"We need some eyes and ears in that area. Someone that doesn't look like a typical wildlife law enforcement officer. We need some tips that will lead us to those dirty crooks."

"I think I can do that."

"Don't jump into this too quickly. A couple of decades ago most poachers were traditional mountain folk looking to supplement their meat supply. That's changed. Nowadays there's some big money involved; this could be a dangerous assignment. When one trophy head can go for tens of thousands of dollars, imagine how much money a couple of dozen trophy heads would be worth. People trying to stop this business could well be risking their lives."

"So you really think this is dangerous?"

"If you get into a situation where the poachers think you could jeopardize their operation, things could get really ugly."

"I understand; OK, what can I do to help?"

"Go back to your ranch job and simply watch for any suspicious activity. Do you remember Mikel, that old Basque sheepherder?"

"Of course, we visited him once when I went with you to inspect some beaver dams, and also I stayed with him for a while when I worked on the project to study interactions between sheep and wildlife."

"He lives full time with his dogs west of Grand Lake. He might have noticed some suspicious activities. Maybe if you get a chance, you can pay him a visit sometime. Do you have transportation?

Jane replied, "In the past I've managed to find something on the CSU ride board. There's also a bus to Denver, and I can get to Grand Lake from there."

Bill thought for a moment,"I'll tell you what. I have an old jeep I could lend you. It's not pretty, but I recently had it serviced, and it's dependable; I rarely use it anymore. Your aunt has been after me to get it out of the yard next to the driveway before the neighbors complain. I mostly use a motor pool vehicle anyway, and I have your Aunt Ronda's car for personal trips. If you get a little money ahead, I could sell it to you for a reasonable price."

"I do have a couple of thousand in my savings account."

"How about if I sell it to you for $150?"

"Well, I think that would be stealing from you, but I'd rather not worry about driving around in a borrowed car."

"Actually, it would make someone in my house happy to see it go. She was threatening to pay someone to haul it away. Let's make a deal. If you can hang around until I'm through work today, you can stay at our house tonight and we'll finalized the deal tomorrow. Your aunt will be happy to see you, and our spare room is always there for you.

"By the way, don't tell your aunt about becoming a spy for the department. She'd only try to talk you out of it, and the fewer people who know about it the better. I trust your aunt, but I'm suspicious that somehow things are getting out from our department to the poaching organization.

"Also, don't tell anyone you got the jeep from me. You don't want to show any connection with my department."

Jane frowned, "How am I going to explain how I suddenly have a new jeep?"

"OK, here's a cover story. Say you were checking the ride board at the Lory Union, and you saw a guy... say he looked like he was from the Middle East, who was posting a for sale sign for a jeep, and the price seemed to be too low to be true. When you asked him about it, he explained he had been supported by his family for a number of years, and they decided he was not making enough progress toward a degree. They were pulling his funding, and he had to return home immediately. So, you negotiated on the price and got an impossible deal on the jeep."

The next day, Jane and Bill went to the county records office and officially transferred the title to the jeep into Jane's name. Jane then thanked Uncle Bill with a hug and headed for Grand Lake.

There is no quick way to get from Ft. Collins to Grand Lake. The quickest way timewise is to go south to Denver, then over Berthod pass and down through Winter Park. Jane hated the traffic around Denver and was not in any hurry, so she dismissed that route. Another option is to take 287 north to Laramie, Wyoming, and then loop back through Walden, Colorado. Or, she could take Colorado 14 up the Poudre River Canyon, cross the continental divide and take 27 down through Rand. The longest option timewise is to go south to Loveland, up the Big Thompson Canyon to Estes Park, enter Rocky Mountain National Park, and then take Trail Ridge Road over the divide. Since she was not on any time schedule, Jane decided to take the scenic Rocky Mountain National Park option.

No matter how many times you make the trip, the drive over Trail Ridge Road is always a thrill. The route from Ft. Collins to Loveland is too close to the mountains to actually see much of the back range. Then as you head up the Big Thompson Canyon, the mountains close in. As you pass through Estes Park, however, the snow covered peaks reveal themselves and Long's Peak, at over 14 thousand feet, is the king of the neighborhood. Of course, Long's Peak is only one of over 50 Colorado mountains that reach that high.

Outsiders get confused by the different uses of the word 'park.' Rocky Mountain National Park is what you expect a park to be, a preserved and public area. Estes Park, however, is a geological park. A geological park is a relatively flat area surrounded by mountains. Estes Park is only a few miles across while North, Middle, and South Parks in Colorado cover hundreds of square miles.

On the west side of Estes Park, Jane entered Rocky Mountain National Park. From the Beaver Meadows entrance, she followed Rt 36, left the Big Thompson Creek valley, and headed up Trail Ridge Road, the highest continuous highway in the US. At the highest point, it's over 12 thousand feet in elevation. At Milner Pass, the road crosses the continental divide and drops back down in elevation to Grand Lake, at around 8 thousand feet.

Driving up Trail Ridge Road, Jane was aware that the climate in the mountains is completely dependent on elevation. On a summer's day in Ft Collins, which

is around 5 thousand feet, it might be 80 degrees. At the same time on Trail Ridge Road, it might be snowing. As the road climbs to the Trail Ridge Road summit, it passes through the timber line at around 11 thousand feet. Above that level, there are no trees, only very low growing plants that are also found in the far north in the tundra.

As Jane drove her newly acquired jeep through the mountains, she sucked in the crisp clean mountain air she loved. The wildflowers seemed to be nodding their heads to welcome her back. Small groups of elk were grazing on the fresh summer grass, some right next to houses in Estes Park. As she passed by her old research area at Sheep Lakes, she spotted a herd of big horn sheep crossing the road, stopping traffic and amazing tourists. She stopped several times to take short hikes and admire the surroundings.

It was early evening when Jane arrived back at the cabin where she was staying while working part-time at a ranch. After unpacking, she went to the office to let them know she was back, and found her friend Nancy working the front desk.

"Howdy, stranger," Nancy greeted her. "I'm glad to see you back. How was the big train trip to Chicago?"

"The trip was fine, and thanks again for dropping me at the station in Granby. I'm afraid my visit with my friend Janice could have been better."

"I thought you two were best friends in college."

"We were. It just seems that our interests have changed and we've moved in different directions. I'm still an unsophisticated mountain girl while Janice is now a city woman preoccupied with the latest fashions. She even insisted I dress up in a manner she approved, instead of my typical shirt and jeans. Can you imagine me in spike heels, a mini skirt, a frilly blouse, and Frederick's of Hollywood underwear running to catch a train?"

"I'm trying to picture that, and in my mind I admit it looks pretty funny."

"Well that's the picture. Janice insisted that I dress up to her standards, and I couldn't bring myself to refuse. On my way to the train, I slipped and would have sprawled all over the platform, but I fell against a guy who managed to stop my fall. I don't think of myself as clumsy, and I was so embarrassed, I hurried to the train without even thanking him."

"So how was the train ride?"

"The story gets worse. The Janice costume kept feeling dumber and dumber. I just had to get out of it, and finally went into the toilet to change. Just when I had stripped down to nothing, a guy opened the door."

"No, don't tell me you forgot to lock it?"

"I'm afraid so."

"Did the guy get a good look?"

"I was so startled, I screamed and called him a pervert; he closed the door and told me to lock the door if I didn't want visitors."

"Sounds like you had your share of embarrassing moments."

"The guy was actually kind of nice. He sat beside me later and teased me. He claimed he was not really a pervert, but that I might well be an exhibitionist. Not only that, it turns out that he was the one I fell into on the train platform."

"Was this guy an old fart, or was he a real hunk?"

"He's probably close to my age, and not too bad to look at. We talked for a while, and then there was a freight train wreck that shut down the train for a couple of days."

"That does not sound like fun. So then what did you do for a couple of days?"

"I didn't have enough cash for a motel. There was only one room left in the motel, and I shared it with Andrew, the guy who opened the door on me."

"Don't tell me you actually slept with this Andrew fellow!"

"Well, not really."

"What do you mean 'not really'? Either you slept with him or you didn't."

"OK, we shared the honeymoon suite, and we slept in the same bed, but I can't actually say I 'slept' with him."

"The honeymoon suite? This story keeps getting better and better."

"That was the only room left at the Wigwam Motel. You can't believe what it was like. It even had a heart shaped hot tub."

"I am having a hard time with this. You flash a stranger on a train, then you spend a couple of days with him in a honeymoon suite. Were you on drugs or something?"

"No! It all just sort of happened. Andrew was a perfect gentleman. We built a row of pillows between us. He treated me with complete respect. He never even tried to feel me up."

"Did you want him to... 'feel you up'?"

"No!... I don't know. It doesn't matter now anyway. The wreck was cleared away, the train continued, and we went our separate ways."

"It looks like you haven't quite gotten over your storybook 'stranger on a train' adventure. Of course, in the storybook version you would have gotten married and lived happily ever after."

"We did get married... sort of."

"Come on! How can you 'sort of' get married?"

"There was this nice old lady at the reception desk, Andrew called her 'Aunt Martha' because she reminded him of someone he knew. Anyway, when we arrived at the motel, I went to make a phone call to arrange to get some money wired to tide me over while Andrew went to check in. 'Aunt Martha' assumed we were a married couple. Since there was only one room left, he let her believe we were together and took the room. He gave me the option of backing out of the arrangement, but there were no more rooms, and I didn't have enough cash, so I let him talk me into it."

"So you spent a couple of days pretending to be husband and wife?"

"Yes... It just seemed easier that way. And Andrew was so nice and polite about everything. He even paid for the room and our meals, and refused my offer to send him a check when I got back home. He claimed we had been married by 'Aunt Martha', and since we were married, his money was our money."

"After all of that, you just let him ride off into the sunset?"

"In retrospect I can think of all the things I should have done differently. But it's over now, and I just have to get on with my life. I know I will. Even now it seems like something that happened to someone else."

---

Jane resumed her normal duties at the ranch and thought about ways she might do some poacher spying for Uncle Bill. One of the things on her duty list was cleaning the swimming pool. She looked at her old swimsuit and found the lining was falling apart. The Grand Lake general store served the tourist market and had a little of everything on the shelves including swimsuits.

On her next day off, she collected Nancy and suggested a trip to Grand Lake for a little shopping.

"I'll drive," Jane said, "You can check out my new jeep."

"Where did you get this? I thought your bank account was reserved for graduate school."

"I wasn't planning to buy a car. When I was in Ft Collins, I was checking the CSU ride board, and this mid-eastern looking guy was putting up a for sale poster. I got talking to him, and he said his family was fed up with sponsoring him as a professional student, and he had to return home immediately. He had to get rid of his jeep quickly or just abandon it in a parking lot somewhere. He made me an offer I couldn't refuse, and I bought the jeep from him."

"You just must be living right these days. First you meet a sugar daddy on the train who pays all of your expenses, and then you meet some Arabian Prince who gives you a car. I can't believe it."

They got into the jeep, and set off for the Grand Lake general store. Jane and Nancy looked through the collection of swimsuits. Jane selected a black one piece; Nancy found a red bikini left over from the spring break collection that was marked 50% off.

"Check this out, Jane. Half price. How can you resist."

"Not my style, I'm afraid."

"Come on. Loosen up a little. You're already the harem girl of some Arabian Prince. You might as well dress for the part."

"Let's see if there is somewhere I can try them on."

Jane went to the counter where she found her friend Sue in charge.

"I'd like to try on these swimsuits before I decide which one to buy. Is there any place I could try them on?"

"We don't have an official changing room, but if you don't tell Jerry, the boss, I can unlock the custodians' closet for you. It's a little small, so be careful."

"Nancy, could you maybe watch out for me and keep anyone from peeking?"

"OK, but I doubt that will be a problem."

Sue unlocked the closet for Jane, and Nancy stood guard until a couple of customers lined up at the checkout counter. Sue called over to Nancy and asked her if she could help with a price check.

There wasn't much room to maneuver, and Jane had to struggle to undress in the small space. She dropped a swimsuit on the floor, and as she was reaching down to pick it up, her butt bumped the door, which swung open. As she turned to close it, she caught a glimpse of a man she was sure must be staring right at her. She shrieked, grabbed the door, and said, "Damn! Not this again."

Through the closed door she imagined she heard someone say 'exhibitionist'. Or, maybe she really heard it. Or not.

Nancy came back to see how she was doing.

"What do you think of the red one?"

"I think the black one is more my style. Did you see someone staring at me when I accidentally bumped the door open?"

"Why, were you flashing someone again?"

"No. I probably imagined it."

"Why not take both suits? The price is right."

"Maybe I will. I have to clean the pool and sometimes I need to get into the water to clean the drains. I'm a little self conscious because my skin is so pasty; I look like I'm an albino or something."

"Why not do a little sunbathing during your break?"

"I hate to have the guests see me laying around. I can just feel their beady eyes checking me out."

"You need to get on a horse, and ride out to some secluded spot where you can sunbathe in private."

"Well, maybe I'll give that some thought."

Jane went over to the counter to pay Sue for her purchase.

"Did you see a strange man over by the closet door when I was changing?"

"I don't know about any strange men. A guy did come in to buy some camping supplies. He was riding a bike from your ranch, said he was a freelance photographer here to do some hiking and nature photography. Why do you ask? Looking for a new boyfriend?"

"Never mind. I just thought some pervert might have been spying on me when I was trying on the swimsuits. I guess I'm a just a little paranoid after my train trip."

"What happened on the train?"

"It's a long story. A guy opened the toilet door on me when I was changing. I guess I have a thing about men peeking at me."

Jane paid for the purchase and found Nancy checking out the magazine covers. They headed back to the ranch.

The morning sky the next day was bright and cloudless. In the high country, it was not unusual to see the temperature change 40 or 50 degrees in a 24 hour period. When the sky was clear, the sun could move the thermometer from close to freezing to a pleasant 70 degrees in a few hours. Jane decided this was a good day to try to work on a tan.

Thinking to find a private place for sunbathing, she saddled up Starburst, the horse she usually rode. Starburst was temperamental and didn't like strangers. As a result, Starburst was not used on the regular trail rides. Most of the people who came to the ranch for horseback riding were not experienced riders. They didn't have the horsemanship skills it took to get Starburst to accept them. This meant she was available to Jane and some of the other staff who could take the time to make friends with Starburst.

Jane directed Starburst up the Kawuneeche Valley, and left the trail when she found a small meadow surrounded by trees and hidden from sight by anyone hiking on the Colorado River trail.

She removed an old saddle blanket she had brought, spread it on the ground, and stripped down to her new bikini. She smeared on a layer of sunscreen and stretched out on the blanket, and with the warm sun on her back, soon fell asleep.

## Chapter 11 - Andrew Arrives in Colorado

At the Omaha station, Andrew boarded the train for Colorado. The train would take him through Denver, into the mountains passing under the continental divide, through the Moffat Tunnel, and he would get off the train at Granby. This was the closest he could get by train to Lulu City and Elk Park Ranch, where he hoped he would find the packages he'd shipped earlier.

The travel time from Omaha to Denver was over eight hours. He dug out the books he had picked up in Chicago. One told the history of Colorado. The Spaniards explored from Mexico to as far as Kansas in the 1500's, and laid claim to most of the southwest, including Colorado. Colorado had only become a state in 1876, on the 100th anniversary of the establishment of the United States. As a result, Colorado was called the Centennial State. During the gold rush of 1859, the population of the area had increased enough to justify creating a new state by splitting off a piece of the Territory of Kansas. This was only a couple of years before Arvid Jonsson had headed west to strike it rich.

As he read the area history, Andrew decided to leave the train at Julesburg, Colorado, take some time to stretch his legs, and work out the kinks that had developed during the long ride. He also wanted to get a feel for the area he had been reading about. Finding a motel within walking distance of the train station, he checked in and then had dinner at a nearby cafe.

Julesburg is on the South Branch of the Platte River, and in the days of travel by stage coach and when mail was sent via the Pony Express, it was an active place. At the time Arvid had traveled west, trains had replaced stage coaches, and highway travel had reduced Julesburg's importance to travelers.

Andrew was interested in exploring the area Arvid had probably passed through, and tried to imagine what life was like in those days. After breakfast the next day, Andrew visited a museum and immersed himself in local history. He learned about Jack Slade, the infamous operator of several stage company offices, including one in Julesburg. Slade was known as a vicious killer, and was feared by most everyone who came in contact with him. Mark Twain featured a meeting with Slade in his book Roughing It. Slade was killed in 1861, not that many years before Uncle Arvid arrived in Colorado.

Andrew had heard about the Pony Express, and only knew the romantic stories about daring young riders. Now, however, he was at one of the places where these young riders actually passed through. There was really not much romantic about the life of Pony Express riders. They were not, as Andrew had imagined, freewheeling cowboys riding spirited cow ponies.

The riders were young, and physically built like race horse jockeys. Weight was a problem, so everything was kept as light weight as possible. The horses had racing type saddles, minimum saddle blankets, and the riders did not carry guns. The goal was to move mail between the east

PONY EXPRESS

St. JOSEPH, MISSOURI to CALIFORNIA
in 10 days or less.

☛ WANTED ☜

YOUNG, SKINNY, WIRY FELLOWS not over eighteen. Must be expert riders, willing to risk death daily.
Orphans preferred.
Wages $25 per week.

APPLY, PONY EXPRESS STABLES
St. JOSEPH, MISSOURI

and the west coast as fast as possible. The stations

were spaced 10 miles apart. When a rider got to a
station, he would switch horses and gallop on as
quickly as possible. Letters moved from Missouri to
California in 10 days, much faster than alternatives
which took weeks or months. The Pony Express only
operated for two years before it was replaced by the
telegraph and trains.

Andrew spent as much time as he could soaking
up the local atmosphere and trying to imagine what it
must have been like when Arvid traveled through the
area. Too soon, he had to walk back to the station and
board the next train west. Although he planned to ride
the train to Granby, he couldn't resist making a stop in
Denver. He took a taxi from Union Station to the
historic Brown Palace Hotel. It was expensive, but he
decided to splurge a little before heading into the
mountains. From the hotel, it was easy to visit the
wealth of Denver museums.

After exploring Denver, Andrew caught the train
to Granby. Since it was only about 15 miles from
Granby to Elk Park Ranch, he called the ranch office,
and they sent Ned, one of the ranch hands, to pick him
up.

"Welcome to the High Country." said Ned. "Is this
your first visit?"

"Yes, it is. The mountains are truly spectacular.
Even bigger and better than I imagined."

"No mountains where you're from?"

"We have the Appalachians, but they're little hills compared to this."

"I see you're booked for a long stay. What's your plan?"

"I'm trying my hand at doing some freelance photography, mostly nature shots. Maybe I'll try to find some big game, but nothing is too small for me to shoot."

"Well, you picked a good place. You know we're within walking distance of Rocky Mountain National Park. Some good hiking trails start just up the road."

"Yes, I've studied some maps, and it's one of the reasons I picked this place."

"Well, good luck. If you need anything, just let me or one of the staff members know. We get a lot of visitors; many just come for our horseback rides. We also have some mountain bikes available, and we even offer guided nature hikes. A schedule is posted in the lodge office."

Since he had made his reservation and prepaid for a two months stay, Ned took him directly to cabin #7 and handed him his key. It was a rather rustic looking log cabin; Andrew

entered and observed that in spite of the rough looking exterior, the interior had been nicely modernized. He was pleased to see the boxes he had shipped earlier stacked in a corner near the front door. He unpacked and organized everything.

Andrew then took a walk around the ranch and bumped into Ned who gave him a brief tour of the ranch building complex and facilities. He asked Ned if there was a store nearby where he could pick up some camping supplies since there were a few things, mostly like trail food, that he had not shipped ahead.

Ned nodded, "There's a general store in Grand Lake that probably has most anything you need. If you don't mind a hike, it's about 4 miles from here. If you prefer, the ranch has several bicycles available for guest use. You can check out a bike at the office."

"Thanks, Ned. I came here for hiking in the mountains, so a few miles isn't a problem for me. I've also done some trail biking back east, so I'll probably check out the bikes."

Andrew found a collection of bikes in a parking rack beside the ranch office. He went in and introduced himself to the lady on duty at the desk.

"Hi, I'm Andrew Olofsson. I just got in a little while ago. Ned gave me my key and a quick tour around."

"Welcome to Elk Park Ranch. I'm Marge, the owner; I'm the one who took your registration. I see you plan to stay with us for a while."

"Well, I might be in and out. I expect to do some back country hiking, and maybe a little camping. I plan to use this as my base. Thank you, by the way, for putting the packages I sent in my cabin. I had a few things I didn't want to haul along on the train. I bought one of those train passes that lets you get on and off at different stops."

"I hope you had an interesting train ride. It's a long ride from the east coast and some people think it's boring."

"My trip was great. Even the train wreck made it interesting."

"Train wreck? That doesn't sound like fun."

"Actually the train I was on didn't wreck. A freight train on the track ahead of us crashed through a bridge, and it took a couple of days before our train could move ahead."

"I suppose that the delay interfered with your trip."

"Actually, the delay was the best part of the trip. But I'd rather not talk about it too much."

"OK, I won't ask. Let me explain the procedures here. We have a bulletin board where we post the scheduled activities and sign up sheets. Some guests like to take advantage of horseback rides, barbecue nights, nature hikes, or other things. There's a breakfast buffet every morning in the Green Mountain Room. We offer eggs and bacon, pancakes and cold cereal.

"See these pigeon holes here by the desk? There's one for each cabin. You'll find mail or messages in your pigeon hole. We have mountain bikes for the use of our guests. You can take a bike key from the key board, use it for the bike lock, and put the tag from the bike you're using in your pigeon hole so we know who has which bike.

"The literature rack by the door has hiking trail maps, brochures, and info sheets from local businesses."

"It looks like you have things pretty well organized."

"We've been in business for quite a few years, and have a pretty well developed system. Some customers have been coming here for years, and that's a pretty good recommendation."

"I'd like to check out a bike and take a ride to the general store in Grand Lake that Ned told me about."

"No problem. Use the bike lock whenever you park the bike. Our bikes have all been painted a special color to make them easy to identify; occasionally one of the tourist kids from town decides they need to have a joy ride."

"Thanks a lot, Marge. I think I'll enjoy my stay here."

"We hope you will. Let us know if you need anything."

On the way out, Andrew studied the items in the literature rack and picked out a couple of hiking trail maps. Finding the bike rack, he selected a bike with a large front mounted basket, took the tag, put it in his pigeon hole, and headed for Grand Lake.

The town of Grand Lake is on the shore of... you guessed it, Grand Lake. Gates separate the waters of Grand Lake from Shadow Mountain Lake, about three times larger than Grand Lake. Shadow Mountain Lake is a man-made reservoir on the west slope of the continental divide. Water from Shadow Mountain Lake is diverted through a tunnel to the east slope of the continental divide where it enters the Big

Thompson River and fills a series of reservoirs that dot

what was once desert land and are used to irrigate crops on the east side of the Rockies. Since most of eastern Colorado would be desert without irrigation, water laws are very important. When a drop of water falls in the mountains, how it's decided if it should go west to the Pacific or east to the Mississippi, is very confusing.

Andrew had no problem finding the general store, but he decided to cruise around town before shopping, just to get a feel for the place. Since he expected to be in the area for a while, he wanted to be familiar with the town layout.

Although not especially large, the general store had a good variety of items on display. The lady behind the counter greeted him as he entered.

"Hi. I don't remember seeing you here before. My name is Sue. Can I help you find anything?"

"I'm Andrew. I'm staying at the Elk Park Ranch for a while, and am really looking for some camping supplies like freeze dried food, or gorp. I'd like to browse around and see what all you carry."

"The camping supplies are over in aisle five. Feel free to look around. You'll probably be surprised at what all we carry. We get everybody from local customers, to tourists, to serious campers and hikers. We try to accommodate all their needs. If we don't carry something, we can order it from Denver and have it in a couple of days."

Picking up a small basket, Andrew browsed. In the camping section he found trail mix, energy bars, and a selection of freeze dried meals. He picked up enough to last a couple of days on the trail and added some junk food snacks and canned drinks for evenings at the ranch. He also added a book about hiking in Rocky Mountain National Park for his basket.

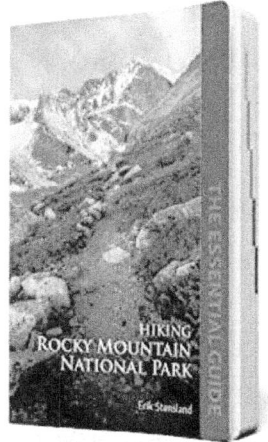

As he was checking out an assortment of fishing gear back in aisle eight, he noticed a door in the far wall swing open, caught a glimpse of some bare skin, and heard a quiet frustrated voice say 'damn!' as the door slammed shut. He had a flashback to his experience on the train, and shook his head.

As he checked out, he said, "I think you have someone hiding in the closet back there."

"That's just the broom closet; sometimes we use it as a changing room. Thanks for your business; hopefully we'll see you again."

"I'm sure you will. I'm staying at the Elk Park Ranch for a couple of months, so I'll be around for a while."

"Are you here for the horseback riding?"

"No, I'm a freelance photographer, I'm going to explore the mountains and see if I can catch some big game, or maybe a wild flower or two."

"Good luck!"

Andrew loaded his purchases into the bike basket and rode back to his cabin. As he studied the mountains, he could see the tree line that Farley had told him about. He had expected to see some snow on the peaks, but there was more than he had imagined there would be.

After parking the bike and returning the bike lock key to the board in the office, he saw Marge, who asked him if he'd found the general store.

"No problem. I'm surprised at the variety of goods they carry. I managed to find some freeze dried food I wanted for doing some backpacking. Tomorrow, I'm planning to do a little exploring. I might be out for a couple of days, so don't worry if you don't see me around."

"It's a big country out here, and it can be easy for folks not used to the mountains to get lost. If you want, I could probably arrange for a guide for you."

"I've done quite a bit of back packing back east, so I'm not completely new at this. I also have a good map collection that should keep me straight."

"OK, just be careful. It's easy to get yourself in trouble if you get off the marked trails."

"Thanks. I'll take it easy and try to keep out of trouble."

Andrew went back to his cabin and spread out his maps.

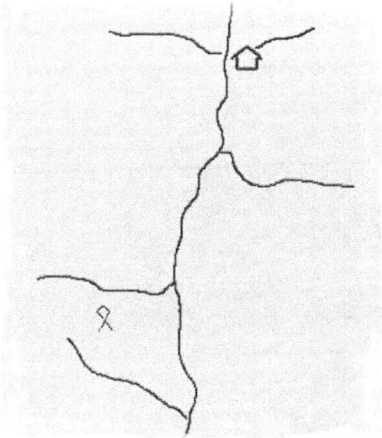

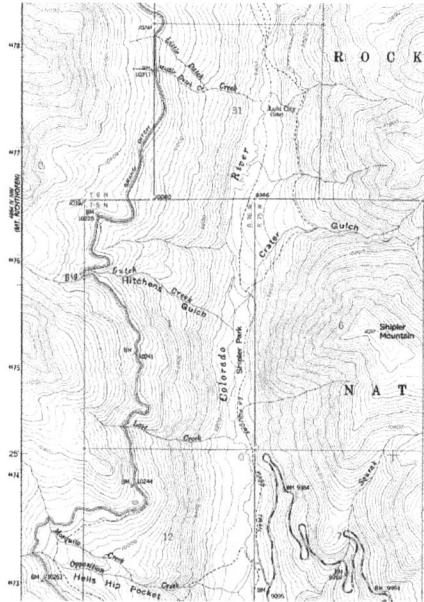

He laid the Arvid map side by side with the USGS topographic map of the area. Once again he convinced himself that Arvid's map replicated the stream pattern on the USGS map. He put a mark on the USGS map corresponding to the location of the symbol on Arvid's map.

He got out the pack frame he had shipped ahead, and loaded the pack with things he would need for a couple of days of hiking. He planned to set out the first thing the next the morning to visit the Lulu City site.

## Chapter 12 - Poachers on the Move

Tex Frey had just finished another round of golf at his country club and went to the dining room where he met with Jim Rogers who told him that he'd been thinking more about a hunting trophy. Rogers had turned a multi million dollar inheritance into a large real estate company in Wichita Falls, eventually opening branches in Dallas and Houston. Originally, he had specialized in buying older apartment buildings and renovating them using urban renewal grants, then renting them to middle and lower income people and spending a minimum on maintenance.

Rogers was a good self promoter, and by paying freelance writers to publish articles about what a smart and successful real estate developer he was, he'd built a reputation. By exaggerating the size of his portfolio, he managed to get large bank loans to first acquire several hotels around Texas, and then to develop several condominiums and golf resorts.

Rogers told Tex that he wanted to know more about a hunting trip to Colorado, and asked Tex if he could meet him at his office to discuss details. Tex smelled money, and agreed to meet him the next day.

Rogers opened the discussion by mentioning that he admired the trophies several of their friends had collected on hunting trips Tex had arranged.

"Oh, you've seen some of those trophies?" Tex asked.

"Yes, I have. I especially like the mule deer head that Jack Miller has in the great room of his retreat on Lake Texoma. I sure would like to have something like that for my vacation cottage. I think a big horn sheep would look great there."

"Trophy big horn sheep heads are not easy to find. They're a lot harder than mule deer. It requires hiring a special guide and scouting the territory for sometimes a month or so before a good trophy can be located."

"Gee, I don't know if I can take off for a whole month."

"We can arrange for a guide I know up in Colorado to do some research in advance. That way the time you would have to be away would be minimized. Of course, we would have to reimburse the guide for his research time."

"How does this work then? You get your guide to scope out a decent trophy, and then he sets up the hunt?"

Tex nodded, "That's right. Once a trophy has been located, the guide lets me know. Then I'll arrange for the trip to Colorado. I know a place where we can stay for a couple of days, and maybe play some cards along the way. After the kill is made, I'll even arrange for a taxidermist to mount the head for you."

"Can your guide find a way for me to not have to hike up and down a mountain for this? I'm not in shape for much mountain climbing."

Tex winked, "Yes, that's possible. Of course we have to insure that no one will ever know how much actual hunting and shooting you were involved in."

"And just how do you do that?"

"For the right price, my guide will swear to just how much trouble you had to go through to make the kill. He and I have had quite a lot of experience with this, if you know what I mean."

"How much do you think this will cost?"

"This won't be cheap. If you're not ready to spend some serious bucks, just forget about it. There are travel expenses, not only for you, but for the guide and his helper. We'll have to pay for the guide's research time and expenses. There may be horses to rent, and there will be transportation and taxidermy fees. And then there is the consulting fee I'll have to charge for making all of the arrangements."

"I don't see money as a problem as long as you can guarantee a decent trophy. How much are we talking here?"

"I think the project can be undertaken for around $40,000 dollars. That includes the local guide and helper, transportation, taxidermy costs, and my consulting fee."

Jim Rogers sat back, puffed on his cigar, sipped his whiskey, and asked, "Can you really guarantee that I'll end up with a great trophy?"

"Here's the deal. If you're willing to front end the $40,000, in cash, I'm willing to promise a full refund if your 'hunt' is not successful."

"Let me think about this overnight. I have to find ways to finance this thing. I'll give you a call tomorrow and let you know if we have a deal."

"OK, I'll be waiting for your call."

They shook hands, and Tex could tell from the look in Jim's eye that he had a new hunting project. Most of the time in the past, he would let Butch Brown, his go-to-guide, handle the hunting. But, although he had participated in a number of these hunts in the past, he had not bagged a big horn sheep lately. He felt the urge to get a big horn in his sights.

The next day, Tex got a call from Jim Rogers.

"The hunting trip deal is on."

"OK, here's what you do. You put the cash, assorted bills no bigger than $100, in a brief case, and have a courier deliver it to one of my agents. Here's the address."

"It will take a couple of days to put that together. How soon do you need it?"

"You do what you have to do. When I have the cash in hand, I'll start the project rolling. Once the arrangements in Colorado have been made, I'll contact you with a schedule for your hunting trip."

"Done!" Rogers replied.

Two days later, Tex got a call from his agent confirming that the briefcase from Jim Rogers had been delivered. Tex retrieved the briefcase, contacted his accountant and arranged for of the money to be transferred to his account in the Bahamas. He kept out $5,000 to be used to pay his Colorado team.

Tex put in a call to Dante's Bar in Frisco, Colorado, and asked for Vinnie. When Vinnie got on the phone, he said, "This is your hunting friend from Texas. Could you get word to Butch to call me?"

"Yeah! I'm pretty sure he'll be here tonight. If he doesn't show, I think I know how to find him."

"Thanks!"

"Are we gonna see you soon? There's a couple of whales in town that are looking for a high stakes game."

"It looks like I might have something working soon. I'll be in touch."

Later that night Butch Brown called Tex.

"I got the word you're looking for me. What's up?"

"We've got a customer. I don't want to discuss this over the phone. Can you meet me in Aspen tomorrow?"

"Sure. What time?"

"I'll be at the regular place early in the afternoon."

"All right."

―――――――――――☞―――――――――――

Tex made a call to 'YourJets' and arranged for a Citation X to pick him up at Eisenhower Airport in Wichita Falls and fly him to Sardy Field in Aspen, returning the same day.

When Tex got to the Puma Bar in Aspen, he found Butch sitting in a booth near the back of the room. He nodded to Butch and slid into the seat across from him.

"So what kind of deal do we have this time?"

"I've got a guy who wants a big horn for his 'little' vacation cottage. He's a big spender, but he's not looking to spend a lot of time climbing mountains."

"That's a good thing. I don't like dragging your Texas fat cats through the woods."

"You have any locations that come to mind?"

Butch nodded, "I can think of a place with a good collection of heads. On the west side of Rocky Mountain National Park, up behind Specimen Mountain, there's a nice flock. Since they're protected there, they don't get any hunting pressure and they're not too spooky, and they grow big.

"It can be a little dicey because the area is close to where hikers or tourists might show up. But the area does have fairly easy access if we're careful."

"Sounds good. I haven't had a chance to get a big horn lately, so I want to be in on the kill. Do you have everything you need to set this up?"

"We'll need someone to help with the hauling. I think I can get Luis Sandoval to do the grunt work. He has a kid to feed and I know he's hungry for work."

"Can we trust him?"

"I've used him a couple of times. He's fairly solid, and he knows that if he crosses me, his family will suffer. Yeah, we can trust him."

"Do we need any horses?"

"I think we should get in and make the kill. Then we'll know if we can pack it out. If not, we'll hide the head and come back later with a pack horse. We need to dress like typical back packers in case we meet anyone along a trail. We can switch to camo gear when we get close to the target."

"When can we move on this?"

"Sometime soon. I'll get things together and call you when we're ready to go."

Tex made the trip back home. The next day, he contacted Rob Role, the taxidermist who operated out of Manassa, an isolated town in the San Luis Valley in southern Colorado. Manassa, at 7,600 feet in elevation, and with a population of less than 1,000, was a good place to practice taxidermy if you wanted to stay away from nosy neighbors.

Tex called Rob to verify he was still in business, and if he was available to mount a big horn trophy. Rob was not exactly antisocial, more like non social. If you passed him on the street, which was very unlikely, you would think you were back in the days when the only white men in the

mountains were fur trappers. Rob dressed like, and even smelled like he was on his way to a fur trapper rendezvous.

After several tries, Rob finally answered his phone.

"Talk to me," Rob said.

"This is your Texas hunting friend. How's business?"

"What do you have?"

"I'm going to have a big horn head coming in soon. What kind of turn around time can I expect?"

"You still willing to pay double the going price?"

"Of course. Maybe even a bonus for an expedited order."

"Seeing how you've never stiffed me in the past, always pay cash, and the fact that it's not hunting season so business is slow, I could turn it around in about two months."

"Sounds good. I'll be in touch."

Butch contacted Luis Sandoval and put him on notice to stand by for a hunting trip. Although Luis had worked with Butch before, he was not completely comfortable about the idea of poaching, however, he still had some serious bills outstanding from his daughter's hospital stay. A collection agency had been hounding him, and he didn't see any alternative source of funds.

Once Butch had made the necessary arrangements, he called Tex and they decided to meet in three days at 3 AM behind the old ski school building in Winter Park. Tex flew into Denver, rented an SUV, and drove to Winter Park, leaving his rented SUV in a parking lot. He joined Butch and Louis in Butch's pickup truck.

Tex transferred a hard case containing his military style sniper rifle to the pickup. Having recently spent more than a few hours at a shooting range with his Blaser R93, he was confident of his skill. The gun could be broken down to fit in a case not much bigger than a briefcase, and it could be easily and quickly assembled. It was accurate to over 800 yards. Tex had added a scope and a silencer to the package.

Their pickup made the 45 minute drive to a trail head parking lot in the Kawuneeche Valley on the west side of Rocky Mountain National Park. Tex and Luis had medium sized back packs, while Butch had a larger pack frame. They each wore typical well-worn hiking clothes and boots.

They hiked about 2 miles up the Colorado River Trail without meeting any hikers. Leaving the trail, they worked their way up a draw to the northeast. Once they were well out of sight of the trail, they stopped and put on their camo gear. Tex retrieved the rifle case from Butch's back pack, assembled and loaded it. Then they carefully continued their way up the slope until they came to a ridge overlooking the steep side of an 11,000 foot peak.

In most places in the country, an 11,000 foot high mountain would be very noteworthy, In this area, however, it was dwarfed by Specimen Mountain that rose to nearly 13,000 feet just a few miles to the north east. The terrain in front of them dropped abruptly 2,000 feet from the nearby peak to the Colorado River Valley. There was a deep gorge between the opposite mountain and the ridge they were on.

The ridge provided an excellent vantage point for watching any activity on the opposite mountain. Butch had been searching the area for several days before calling Tex to tell him things were ready.

Butch said, "There's been a small group of sheep hanging around on that mountain across the way. Let's scope it out and see if we get lucky today."

Tex replied, "If we shoot a sheep on the face of that mountain, it's likely to fall down into that gorge."

"Exactly. That's the plan. If we can get the sheep to fall just right, we'll have an easier job of getting it out of here."

Louis had been searching the mountain side through his binoculars.

"There they are. I count 9 sheep in the group and there are some good looking horns."

Tex set up the Blaser R93 and studied the sheep through the scope.

"I've got them. Two of them have real good heads. The range is about 300 yards. No wind. No problem."

Tex took aim at the larger of the two rams and carefully squeezed off a shot. The silenced rifle made no more noise then a deer snort. The biggest ram dropped off the edge of the mountain and fell into the gorge. The rest of the herd raised their heads on alert. Tex quickly squeezed off a second shot and a second ram tumbled into the gorge.

"That was good shooting," said Butch. "I can't believe you actually scored a double. That's not done very often."

---

The three of them relaxed while Tex unloaded and disassembled the rifle. Luis, who had been watching the valley for possible hikers said, "We might have a problem. There's someone down there on a horse."

Butch said, "Just stay put. No one can see us from there."

As they watched, the rider turned off the trail and stopped in a small clearing just above the stream, dismounted, and tied the horse.

The three of them got out their binoculars and watched.

"Darned if that ain't a girl," Butch said, "What the heck is she doing?"

"Maybe she just stopped to relieve herself," said Luis.

The girl untied a rolled up horse blanket from behind the saddle and spread it out on the ground. She then stripped down to a bikini, rubbed sunscreen all over herself, and stretched out on the blanket.

Butch said, "Looks like she's doing a little sunbathing. That's a nice show she's putting on for us, but it's gonna be a problem."

"Maybe not," replied Tex." That horse would be very handy for packing out those ram heads. Butch, do you think you could maybe sneak down there and tie up the girl and take the horse? You'd have to be careful so there's no way she could identify you."

"I think we should just sit and watch for a while. How long do you think she's likely to be sunbathing up here?"

"OK, in the meantime let's slowly make our way down closer to our sheep. Butch, you keep an eye on her."

Tex and Luis climbed down into the gorge, found the two sheep, and started removing the heads. Butch moved to where he could keep an eye on the sunbather. When she had been motionless for quite a while, Butch guessed she had fallen asleep.

He removed a pigging string and a ski mask from his pack and crept up silently, jumped on the girl's back and used the pigging string fast as if he was binding a calf for branding. He slipped the ski mask backwards over her head to serve as a blindfold. He took out his knife and cut strips from the saddle blanket she was laying on. Tying her ankles together with the blanket strips, he then retied her hands, removed his pigging string, and then tied her hands and feet together so that she was unable to move. She squirmed around helplessly.

140

He put his mouth close to her ear and said, "Don't hurt yourself struggling. You ain't goin' anywhere. I'll be back in a while and you and me might have a little fun."

Butch then led the horse Starburst to the gulch, and by exchanging whistles, located Tex and Luis. Tex asked what happened to the girl.

"She's tied up like a calf ready for branding. I got her eyes covered so she can't identify us. When we get these sheep heads ready to move, we can go back and decide what to do with her."

"There's too much at stake here to leave any witnesses around. You know what I mean?"

"You mean you want her to disappear?"

"Maybe she might just have a riding accident. It's dangerous to ride in these mountains all alone, you know."

Butch and Luis exchanged a wary glance, but didn't say anything.

Once the ram heads were removed from the sheep carcasses, they were placed in heavy duty garbage bags, draped over the horse's saddle, and tied in place. The horse didn't like the smell of the plastic garbage bags that held the two ram heads, but eventually resigned herself to duty as a pack horse.

"Now let's see to that girl," Tex said.

Butch led then to the place where he was sure he had left her, but she wasn't there.

"I know this is the place," he insisted.

"Well, maybe your memory is not as good as it used to be. She's sure not here. You haven't been sipping on that bottle I know you have in your pack, have you?"

"No! I have not! I swear this is where I left her. I hog tied her with strips from her saddle blanket. There's no way she could get free from that."

"Maybe she had a knife hidden somewhere and cut herself free," Luis suggested.

"She was wearing a bikini, you idiot. Just where do you think she was hiding a stupid knife? Everything she had with her was in the bag that's tied to her horse, and we have that."

"Maybe this isn't the place you left her. Let's look around some."

After they searched the nearby area, Tex observed, "We're wasting too much time. The longer we hang around here the more likely we'll get caught. Butch, are you absolutely sure she didn't see you?"

"She was asleep when I jumped on her back and tied her hands. As soon as I had the ski mask on her head, I got her hog tied real good. There's no way she saw me."

"OK, let's forget about the girl and get out of here."

The three made their way back to the pickup truck. Tex and Butch took the lead while Luis led the now loaded horse. Luck was with them, and they didn't meet any hikers or tourists along the way.

"What do we do about this horse?" Luis asked, stroking and patting the horse. Starburst was getting used to his touch and smell.

Tex thought about it for a minute, "We don't have any way to transport it out of the area. Luis, you wait with the horse back in the woods here until it gets dark. Then ride the horse down toward Grand Lake. Keep out of sight. When you get close to town, tie the horse where it's likely to be found. Then hike to that gas station near the general store and wait there.

"Here's some money. Buy yourself some snacks while you're waiting. You're still wearing those hiking clothes. If anybody asks, tell them you've been hiking and are waiting for your friend to pick you up. After Butch drops me back at my car, he'll come back for you."

Butch and Tex returned to the SUV and transferred the heads. Tex then drove to Dante's Bar in Frisco. Dante's had a couple of rental rooms upstairs, and Tex had stayed there before. He always paid cash and was always welcome. After a few drinks and a visit with Vinnie, he called it a night. The next day he drove south over Hoosier Pass, down through South Park, and continued on south to Manassa where he dropped off the big horn heads.

Rob was a little surprised to see two heads instead of one.

"I thought when you called me you were only talking about one head."

"I was lucky and caught a double."

"I assume you're going to pay a premium for this job, and I suppose you want both of these by yesterday."

"You're correct about the premium, but only the bigger one is a rush job. The other is a bonus, on spec if you will, and you can get it done when you get it done. Here's cash up front for the first one. When you get around to the second one, you'll get more."

With that, Tex drove back to the Denver airport, turned in the rental SUV, and headed for home. On the flight back, he thought about the sheep hunt, and wondered what had happened to the girl Butch had tied up. This was a loose end, and he hated loose ends. He slapped his knee hard and thought, "Dammit, that girl couldn't have gotten loose on her own."

Whoever let her loose was likely a witness. This could blow up his whole Colorado hunting gold mine.

He'd have to get in touch with Butch Brown and have him investigate that stupid sunbather.

Arvid's Treasure

## Chapter 13 - Andrew Takes A Hike

The morning was crisp and clear with a typical intense blue Colorado sky as Andrew shouldered his pack and headed for the Lulu City area.

The trail is on the east side of the Colorado River. Calling it a river at this point does not provide an accurate picture, since in the Kawuneeche Valley it appears as a small stream that meanders through meadows and wetlands. The Colorado River Trail starts with a steep climb up from the valley floor. Andrew thought back to Farley's advice about remembering to breathe as he acclimated himself to hiking at nearly 10,000 feet above sea level. For most of the way to the Lulu City site, the trail ran generally parallel to the river and stayed in the forest. There were occasional breaks between the lodge pole pine trees where Andrew could view the Kawuneeche Valley and the Never Summer Mountains rising to the northwest.

A small sign indicated he had reached the Lulu City site. He recalled the old photos he had seen

while doing his research; they showed a few tumbled down cabins.

The cabins were no longer in evidence. It was hard to imagine that at one time 500 people had lived here. He explored the meadows and woods and tried to find signs of the blacksmith shop where Arvid had worked, but in the nearly a hundred years since Arvid had been here nature had done a good job of taking back the land.

Andrew managed to find the Lulu City cemetery, although the only evidence was a half dozen unmarked stones. It would seem that with a population of up to 500 during the mining rush days of the 1880's, there would have been more graves. There were many stories of bar fights and shootings over claim jumping in these mining towns. Perhaps most of the residents in those days were like Arvid, single men with no local friends or family to worry about taking care of their remains.

Andrew noticed a level scar that traced a line around the side of the mountains. The guide book he'd purchased at the general store explained that the

148

'Grand Ditch' was built in the 1930's to collect water from the Never Summer Mountains. The water was used to irrigate farms 100 miles to the east in what was otherwise desert.

He spent the better part of the day exploring the Lulu City area. He found several decaying piles of logs that must have been miners shacks, and found tailings from old prospects. Several times he came upon old elk and mule deer antlers that, because of the dry conditions, remained for a long time after they had been shed.

He made his way down the west side of the valley and tried to identify the place Arvid had marked on his map. What was shown on the topographical map as streams had no water at this time of the year. There were, however, a few aspen trees mixed in with the lodge pole pines in what looked like dry stream beds. Aspen trees only grow where there is water so it was likely that these dry stream beds had water when the snow was melting.

Andrew climbed a slope that he guessed might be near the area of the mysterious symbol on Arvid's map.

Finding a relatively level place that provided a nice view of the valley, he set up his tent and made a crude meal of trail mix and energy bars. While it was still light enough to read, he studied the guidebook to learn more about the animals and plants of the area.

From his vantage point several hundred feet above the valley, he scanned the surrounding mountainsides and the valley floor using his binoculars. He was amazed at how far he could see in the clean mountain air. This was not at all like the eastern mountains where there was more moisture in the air to limit visibility, and where the terrain was covered with the thick foliage of deciduous trees.

In the evening, a small heard of elk appeared and grazed in the meadows near the river. He also spotted several mule deer as they came down off the mountain to drink from the river. High on a ridge across the valley, he saw a group of big horn sheep. As darkness fell, the stars appeared, a breathtaking sight. More stars than he had ever seen before. Andrew took a deep breath and decided that it just didn't get much better than this.

The next morning Andrew continued scanning the area using the zoom lens on his Nikon camera. He again spotted the group of big horn sheep on the ridge across the valley, and snapped a few

pictures. He examined his topographical map and from the map scale estimated that the sheep were nearly a mile away. Even with his zoom lens, the sheep were not very large in the frame. He guessed he could do some enlarging later and end up with some decent shots.

Suddenly, one of the biggest rams collapsed and fell down into the gulch below. Then, a few moments later, a second ram dropped and also tumbled down the cliff. This startled the rest of the flock and they scampered up the slope and over the ridge out of sight. This was curious! Andrew didn't know much about the behavior of big horn sheep, but he doubted they had a habit of collapsing and falling down a cliff.

He then noticed a horseback rider coming up the valley. Riding to a small clearing surrounded by trees not far from the river, the rider dismounted and pulled something that looked like a blanket from the back of the horse and spread it on the ground. It became clear the rider was a girl when she stripped off her clothes revealing a bikini. A very nice looking woman. She then smeared what Andrew guessed to be suntan lotion over her body, and stretched out on the blanket.

Andrew's day just kept getting more and more interesting. He decided to keep still and watch the show. The lessons learned at the Tom Brown tracker school came back to him. Tom always said that it was movement that made things visible. As Andrew scanned the area where the sheep had been, he detected movement on the ridge opposite where the sheep had fallen. He focused his zoom lens on the area and waited. He eventually detected a figure dressed in camouflage slowly moving down the ridge toward the gulch. Then he spotted two other figures following the first.

Here then was an explanation for the falling sheep. Those guys were hunters. They must have used a silenced sniper rifle to kill the two sheep. This had to be illegal. First of all it was in Rocky Mountain National Park; second, although he didn't know when it was hunting season in Colorado, he was sure there wasn't hunting in June. Those guys must be poachers Andrew decided.

The next question was whether the sunbathing girl was in cahoots with the hunters. Maybe she brought the horse to be used to carry out the bodies of the sheep. Or, more likely, trophy sheep heads. Andrew took a few pictures of the girl on the blanket just in case they could be useful as evidence.

He continued to observe the scene, wondering if, and or how, he should report this. Certainly Ned back at the ranch would know. It also was clear that he had better remain out of sight of the poachers. They might prove dangerous if they knew they had been observed in the act.

One of the poachers drifted away from the other two and stealthily moved toward the sunbathing girl. Andrew wondered if she had fallen asleep.

---

The poacher crept closer to the girl. Then, with a sudden move jumped on her back and tied her hands behind her. He pulled something over her head, and then tied her hands and feet together. The poacher left her laying tied up on the blanket and led the horse away toward the gulch where the other two poachers had disappeared.

Andrew decided he had to help the girl. Moving as quickly as he could, he was careful to conceal himself from view of the gulch where the poachers were last seen.

He approached the girl, put his head near hers, and quietly said, "Please don't be afraid, I'm here to help."

The girl struggled wildly, trying to free herself from the ropes. Her struggles caused her bikini top to slide partially off.

"I'm not the guy who tied you up. If you hold still, I'll cut you loose. If you keep jerking around, I might accidentally cut you."

Andrew used his Swiss army knife to cut the strips of cloth that had been used to bind her. As soon as her hands were free, she pulled off the ski mask her attacker had used to blindfold her.

She looked at her rescuer, "Andrew?"

"Jane?"

"What are you doing here?"

Andrew had already removed the hooded sweatshirt he was wearing and handed it to her to cover herself.

"Let's talk later. We need to get away from here before those guys come back."

"What's going on?"

"I think those guys are poachers. They took your horse, probably to use to haul away the sheep they killed. Let's get up to my tent and hide out for a while."

"Your tent?"

"I'll explain later. Grab your blanket and let's try to remove evidence that you were here. Hopefully they'll be confused about where they left you, and that will give us a little more time to get away."

154

Jane picked up her saddle blanket while Andrew took a dead branch and scraped away their tracks. He led her across the meadow and up the side of the mountain toward his tent. As soon as they were concealed in the trees, Andrew warned Jane to move slowly to avoid detection; he tried to remember what Tom Brown had taught in his tracking books. 'Move when brother wind moves things. Never let your profile look like a person.' They slowly crept up the mountain, ducking behind trees, and crouching behind rocks and logs as they made their way.

Anyone who has spent much time in the Colorado high country knows the weather can undergo dramatic changes. Most people, especially those from the mid west or the east coast say, 'If you don't like the weather, just wait a minute.' But you won't really understand how fast weather can change unless you've experienced a summer day in the mountains. In a matter of minutes, it can go from great sunbathing weather to a cold rainy hail storm. As Andrew and Jane slowly made their way up the side of the mountain, the sky darkened and opened, and a hard rain drenched everything in sight, including the two climbers.

Eventually they reached Andrew's tent. Fortunately, Andrew hadn't bought a bright yellow or blue tent; instead he'd selected one with a camouflage coloring. The flat spot he had chosen to pitch his tent was out of sight from the Kawuneeche Valley, and he was pretty sure that as long as they stayed quiet, the poachers wouldn't find them. The tent was designed for one person, and it was a tight squeeze for Jane, Andrew, and his large back pack.

"I'm afraid we have to get out of these wet clothes," Andrew said, "I don't have much to pick from. Here's a t-shirt, and sweat pants I use for sleeping. Do you want to blindfold me while you change?"

"Don't be silly. We passed that nonsense a long time ago."

As they changed to t-shirts and pants, it was impossible to avoid some serious body contact.

"Now Andrew, can you tell me what's going on and what you're doing here?"

"Do you remember my story about Uncle Arvid?"

"You mean the family treasure legend?"

"Yes. Well, the post mark on the package Arvid sent to the family was Lulu City. And that's what brought me here.

"Yesterday I hiked to Lulu City, looked around for a while, and set up camp."

"Why did you choose this spot?"

"Take a look at Arvid's map. My best guess is that cryptic symbol marks a spot somewhere right around here. This morning I was enjoying the scenery and focused in on a group of big horn sheep on the mountain across the valley from here. Suddenly I saw a big ram fall down into the gorge, and a moment later a second one fell.

"I don't know anything about the behavior of big horn sheep, but this seemed a little strange. As I scanned the ridge across the gorge from where the sheep fell, I saw something move. As I watched through my telephoto lens, I eventually realized that there were three men there moving toward the gulch where the sheep fell.

"Then I saw someone on horseback riding up the valley. I first thought it was someone who was part of the sheep killers' crew bringing a horse to help carry the sheep away. But then one of them sneaked down and attacked you."

Jane groaned, "You mean that you were spying on me when I was sunbathing? Maybe you really are a pervert."

"Look, if a beautiful woman wants to pose for me, how am I supposed to resist? That's my story. Now what's yours?"

"I told you I had a part-time job on a ranch on the west slope. I work at the Elk Park Ranch."

"I can't believe it. That's the place where I'm staying."

"So you are the mystery freelance photographer that the staff has been talking about. But I thought you were a writer."

"Photographer is my cover story. I'm not really employed as a writer anymore, and my friend Farley suggested that it would be better if people didn't know I was a treasure hunter. I'm still not sure why you decided to come way up here for your sunbathing."

"Well, one of my jobs at the ranch is cleaning the swimming pool. Sometimes I have to get into the pool to clean the drains, and it's best if I wear a swimsuit to do that. I haven't been in the sun in my swimsuit enough to develop any sort of tan. I guess I'm a little vain, but I don't want the guests to see me looking like a pale ghost. I also don't like people ogling me when I'm sunbathing. My friend Nancy suggested I take a ride to someplace private to get some sun, and I ended up here. That's the last time I'm going to take Nancy's advice."

"Why is that?"

"Following her advice recently has been a mistake. When she suggested I try on swimsuits in the general store closet, I bumped the door open and made a spectacle of myself to some customer."

Andrew chuckled.

"What's so funny about that?" Jane demanded.

"Don't worry about it. I only saw a quick flash of skin. Not enough to satisfy my pervert instincts."

"You were in the store? What is it that keeps us meeting like this?"

Andrew smiled, "I don't know, but I'm very happy it does. After I left the train in Omaha, I couldn't stop thinking about how I should have acted differently, and how sorry I was that it ended the way it did."

Jane nodded, "I have to admit, I felt the same way."

"The rain has cleared off. Let's take a look and see if there's any sign of the poachers."

Andrew took the Nikon and handed Jane the binoculars. They crept to the viewing place from where Andrew had seen the big horn sheep fall.

"Look, down the valley. There goes my horse. Three men are heading down the trail and one of them is leading Starburst. They must be packing out the ram heads."

Andrew said, "We're certainly not going to catch up with them, and it would probably be stupid to try. I don't think they know anything about me. I have no idea what they would do if they caught you again, but it's unlikely they would offer you a ride home. Is there someone at the ranch we could report this to?"

"I know exactly who to report it to, but he's not at the ranch. You know how you have a cover story to keep people from knowing what you are really up to? Well, I have a secret of my own.

"Do you remember my telling you about my Uncle Bill? He's working on a case trying to close down a major poaching ring. He asked me to keep my eyes open for any suspicious activity in the area. I guess when he hears I fell asleep sunbathing while the poachers were doing their dirty work, I'll probably be fired. Worse than that, my aunt will give us both a tongue lashing that will last until next Christmas. As soon as we get back to the ranch, I'm going to have to give him a call."

"I don't think we will get back to the ranch this evening. It'll soon be night, and we can't hike all the way back to the ranch in the dark. It looks like we'll have to spend the night in the tent. I'm afraid my tent is nothing like room 106. My sleeping bag doesn't include a king sized bed. Do you think we can survive?"

"It's not exactly like we are still strangers on a train. We'll just have to rough it."

They managed to spoon themselves together in Andrew's sleeping bag. Neither of them complained about the arrangement.

———————————————☞———————————————

The next day they made the hike back to the ranch. Jane made the dreaded report call to Uncle Bill. She expected to get a stern lecture.

Bill Rutherfield, answered his phone, "Rutherfield, Wildlife Enforcement Office."

"Hello Uncle Bill, this is Jane."

"Hey Jane, How's it going."

"I have something to report about the poachers."

"What do you have?"

"Yesterday, in the Kawuneeche Valley, poachers shot two big horn rams."

"And you know this how?"

"I was in the area."

Jane steeled herself for what she expected to be a serious Dutch Uncle lecture.

"What do you men, you were in the area?"

"I was out for a ride, and was doing a little sunbathing, and I was jumped by someone who tied me up and stole my horse."

"What? What the heck were you doing sunbathing while chasing poachers?"

"I wasn't chasing poachers. I didn't even know they were in the area. I just went out for a ride. Anyway, I'm fine. A hiker rescued me.

"He's a nature photographer who was watching for game from a position above the valley. He saw two sheep fall off the cliff and into a gulch across the valley from him. He guessed they'd been shot, but there was no gunshot sound. He took some pictures, but he was quite a ways away, so it's not clear if they'll be useful.

"Then he saw me ride up, get off my horse and start sunbathing. I guess the poachers also saw me. Anyway, this hiker guy saw one of the poachers sneak down, tie me up and steal my horse. When the poacher went off to join his friends to pack up the sheep, this guy rescued me.

"We hid from the poachers until dark. This morning we hiked back to the ranch, and that's where I'm calling from."

"Wait a minute. You spent the night there?"

"The hiker had a tent.."

"You spent the night alone in a tent with a strange hiker?"

"Forget about that. The important thing is that your poacher gang just killed two sheep. They probably just took the heads, but I know where the carcasses are."

Bill thought for a minute, "We're going to have to have a serious talk about your reckless behavior later, but this is the first time we have the opportunity to do a quick follow up on a poaching incident. Usually we don't get a carcass report until it's long after the kill. Tell me again where this took place."

"It's in the Kawuneeche Valley, just south of the Lulu City site. I think Andrew can probably pinpoint the location on his USGS map."

"Who is Andrew?"

"He's the guy who rescued me. He is staying here at the ranch."

"You said he has pictures?"

"Yes. I can mail the film to you."

"Don't put the film in the mail. I'll have a State Trooper pick up the film. Let me put you on hold for a minute."

Bill called the State Police Headquarters in Denver, explained the situation, and asked them to dispatch a trooper as soon as possible to the Elk Park Ranch at Grand Lake to pick up a package of film and have it transferred to the State Police forensic lab in Denver for processing. Then he switched back to Jane.

"Does Andrew have any personal pictures on the roll of film?"

"I'll ask him and include a note with the film."

"OK, you need to make yourself invisible to the poachers. Don't talk to anyone about this poacher thing. Do you have a cover story to explain losing your horse?"

"I'll tell people I was mugged by some hiker on the trail and the mugger stole my horse and left me stranded."

"Good. By the way, thank your friend for saving you. He might well have saved your life."

"Believe me, I need to thank him for some other things as well. I hope to find a way to thank him properly."

"I'm not even going to ask what that means. We need to have a serious talk about this later. Right now, I have to make some contacts while the incident is still fresh. You should keep all this under your hat. We don't want to tip off the poachers that we're onto them. You'll be contacted soon by rangers from the NPS."

Bill paused, frowning, "Do you think the poachers can identify you?"

"I doubt it. The one who grabbed me came from behind and pulled a ski mask backward over my head so I couldn't see anything. But since he covered my face, he couldn't see me either, at least not my face."

"I'm really worried about you. These poachers are ruthless. There's a lot of money in this business; if these guys think you are a witness, you could be in trouble.

"Because the kill is still fresh, it's important to move quickly. You should expect to be interviewed by NPS rangers; I've got to make some calls now. By the way, did you get a chance to pay Mikel a visit yet?"

"No, that's still on my list. Bye, Uncle Bill. I'll be careful."

Bill hung up, and Jane gave a little sigh of relief. She expected, however, that she'd be hearing more from Uncle Bill before this was over.

Jane told Andrew about the call. He removed the film from the Nikon and replaced it with a new roll. When asked if he had any personal pictures on the film, he replied that the only pictures on the roll were those he took of the Lulu City site, and the telephoto shots of the animals he saw.

Jane put the film and a note in an envelope and gave it to Marge at the desk with instructions to give it to the state trooper who'd be picking it up.

"What's all this then?" Marge asked.

"I reported the horse thief. There might be useful pictures on the film in this package, and the police want to see them as soon as possible.

Jane and Andrew agreed to meet in the Lodge for breakfast, and then they headed back to their cabins to decompress.

## Chapter 14 - Andrew Talks to the Rangers

The morning after Andrew and Jane got back from their experience with the poachers, Andrew went to the Green Mountain Room for breakfast. On the way past the reception desk, he stopped and studied the brochures advertising local attractions. Picking up information about the Shipler House Museum, he thought it might be a good place to get a better feel for local history.

He spotted Jane already having breakfast in the Green Mountain Room, and she waved for him to join her. Picking up a plate, Andrew made his selections from the buffet and joined her in a booth near the back wall of the room.

"I hope you've recovered from your ordeal with the poachers yesterday."

"Listen, we have to get our stories straight. There must be no mention of poachers. Uncle Bill doesn't want word of that to get out. My story is that I was grabbed by a nasty hiker who tied me up and stole my horse. You were out hiking and found me and helped me get back to the ranch."

"Why not mention the poachers?"

"Uncle Bill and his colleagues have been working on catching a ring of poachers for some time now. He's worried that if we spread information that the poachers are working in this area, it might cause any local connections to be on guard."

"So we shouldn't tell the local sheriff about it?"

"First of all, it happened in the National Park, and law enforcement in the park is handled by the Park Rangers, not the local sheriff. Second, I'm pretty sure you'll be interviewed by the rangers. Bill will be in contact with his NPS connections, so they'll already know about the poaching."

"Do I have to contact a ranger then?"

"No. They have already scheduled an interview with me this morning. As a matter of fact, they will probably show up here before we're finished with our breakfast. If you can stay around for a while, I'll introduce you, that way they won't have to try and track you down."

"I'm not planning any hikes today. I was thinking of visiting the Shipler House Museum."

"That's a good place to go if you're interested in learning more about local history, especially the area mining activities. I know that as a 'nature photographer' you have a special interest in mining." (wink, wink, nudge, nudge)

"My job here at the ranch is part-time, and I'm supposed to put in 20 hours a week so I'm going to be busy the rest of the day after I talk with the rangers.

"Remember, if anyone asks you about the horse stealing, don't mention poachers, except for your interview with the rangers. I told the horse stealing version to Marge at the desk and it'll quickly spread. She thinks you're a big hero for rescuing me. By now, the story is probably all over Grand Lake."

Two men dressed in NPS uniforms approached the table and greeted Jane. Since she had spent a lot of time in the Park doing her freshwater shrimp research for her graduate studies, she knew them both.

"Andrew, meet Ranger Bob and Ranger Joe. Fellows, this is Andrew. He's the one who rescued me from the poachers."

They shook hands all around. Joe asked Andrew if there was a place they could talk after they interviewed Jane about the incident. It was clear that, in typical police style, they wanted to interview them separately.

Andrew said, "I'm in cabin #7, and I'll wait for you there."

After Bob and Joe finished talking to Jane, they found Andrew sitting on a chair on the front porch of cabin #7. They moved two chairs to face Andrew.

Joe opened the interview, "First, tell us your name, where you're from, and how you came to be in the Park when Jane's horse was taken."

"My name is Andrew Olofsson. I'm from Madison, New Jersey. Until recently, I've been working for *Tales, Trails, & Tails* magazine based in New York City. The magazine owner closed the business and left the staff without jobs. Fortunately, he was nice enough to provide his employees with a generous severance package. I decided to do some traveling before looking for a new job."

"Why did you decide on this area. Do you have connections here?"

"I'd heard a lot of stories about Colorado. Farley, one of my colleagues at TT&T, had done several assignments out here. One of his assignments was shooting elk pictures for a naturalist who was doing a study of a herd on Green Mountain. Farley suggested the place where he stayed while on that job was a good base for hiking. So, based on his recommendation, I made a reservation at Elk Park Ranch and found my way here."

"Did you come here looking for a new job?"

"No, I wanted to see if freelance nature photography might be a new career path. Apparently the west side of Rocky Mountain National Park is less crowded and would offer better picture taking opportunities."

"How did you happen to be hiking in the Kawuneeche Valley?"

"Before I left home, and once I decided to follow Farley's suggestion to stay at the Elk Park Ranch, I spent some time studying hiking trails in the area. I've done a lot of assignments in the past for TT&T and I always try to research an area before I go there. I studied the history of Rocky Mountain National Park. In particular, I researched hiking trails. In the process, I discovered Lulu City. I picked up a USGS map and familiarized myself with the trails and terrain.

"Do you always do that kind of research before you go hiking?"

"When you are taking on assignments for a magazine like TT&T, you had best be very well prepared. Silas Redfern, the owner, actually now the former owner, never sent you on an assignment unless he thought you were pretty well prepared. Otherwise you wouldn't last long in the job. Anyway, I have always enjoyed doing research."

"OK, we're convinced you're not the ordinary casual hiker we mostly see around here. We run into a lot of flat landers in our business, and we know what kind of trouble they can get themselves into. They've caused us a lot of grief. Now, tell us about what happened to Jane."

"I had spent most of the day exploring in and around the Lulu City site. I'm amazed a place that once had a population of around 500 or so could completely vanish. I decided to do some off trail camping; I like to avoid crowds. I'm very careful about taking only pictures and leaving only foot prints, so I hope you don't arrest me for not using an official campsite. I doubt that anyone could tell where I camped.

"Anyway, I set up my tent on a shelf several hundred feet above the valley floor. I kept my tent out of sight, but I had a vantage point from which I had a good view of the valley, and I hoped I could get some good pictures."

Bob was making notes, "What kind of camera do you use?"

"I have a Nikon SLR with a 100mm to 300mm zoom lens."

"Good to know. I was afraid that you were going to say you had a trusty Kodak Instamatic."

"In the evening I observed elk grazing in the river bottom and saw some mule deer come down to drink in the river. I also observed some sheep on the ridge across the valley from me. The lighting was not good enough to get any decent pictures, but I hoped to do better in the morning.

"The next morning, I was not ready for another hike yet, so I took it easy. I went back to my viewing point and saw that the sheep were still where they had been the day before. I estimated they were about a mile away."

"And how did you estimate that?"

"Have you heard the old joke about the easterner who was visiting his rancher friend and had trouble estimating distances?"

"You mean... I'm not going to jump across that ditch, for all I know it's a mile wide!" Joe chuckled.

"Yep! I guess you heard it. Well, I didn't want to be like the easterner in the joke. I took out my topographical map, located where I was, and then checked where the sheep were. The map has one mile squares on it, so it was easy to estimate the distance."

"OK, we're convinced."

The rangers nodded to each other, silently communicating that they understood that Andrew was not an average witness and needed to be taken seriously.

"As I was watching through the Nikon, suddenly one of the rams collapsed and dropped far down into the gulch. Then, a few seconds later, a second ram fell into the gulch. The rest of the group then scampered away.

"I confess that I'm no naturalist, and I don't know much about how big horn sheep behave, but this seemed very unusual."

"You didn't by chance take any pictures of this did you?"

"I took a number of pictures, but I didn't get a shot exactly when the sheep fell. By the way, Jane sent the film to her Uncle Bill for processing."

"We're in touch with Bill Rutherfield. He'll be sending copies as soon as the film has been processed. What happened next?"

"I kept watching the area where the sheep had been. I detected movement on a ridge across the gulch from where the sheep had fallen. Eventually, I saw three people, wearing camouflage, slowly moving toward the gulch.

"Then, out of the corner of my eye, I saw someone on horseback riding up the trail. By this time I guessed the sheep must have been shot by poachers. I thought at first that the rider might have been part of the poacher group and had come with the horse to pack out the sheep.

"The rider turned off the trail into a small clearing, got off the horse, spread out a blanket, and was obviously a girl, sunbathing."

Joe and Bob nodded, smiled, and tried to imagine Jane sunbathing.

"I noticed one of the poachers split away from the others and was moving toward the girl. It looked like she had fallen asleep. This third poacher crept up on her, jumped on her back, tied her up, and took off with the horse toward the gulch."

"Did you get any pictures of this?"

"I took some shots before the guy jumped on the girl, but even with the 300mm lens, I didn't get any closeups. Maybe some serious enlarging might be useful. I'm afraid from where I was, I didn't get a good enough view to be able to identify any of them."

"Then what happened?"

"When the poacher was out of sight, I hurried as fast as I could down the slope and cut the girl loose. I was afraid the poachers would appear at any moment, so I convinced the girl, who I now know was Jane, that we should get up to my tent and hide until they were gone. A heavy rain shower caught us before we got to the tent. We took shelter in the tent until it cleared. We went out to my vantage point and saw the poachers far down the trail heading south."

"So how long did you hide in the tent?"

"By the time we saw the poachers leaving, it was too late to hike back to the ranch. We stayed in the tent and made the hike back the next day."

"Did you have a nice time in the tent?"

"That doesn't deserve a comment. Are there any more questions?"

"Can you tell us about where the sheep fell. The poachers probably only took the heads and left the bodies. If we can find the bodies, we might be able to get something useful."

"You mean you want to find the bullets, and that might tell you something about the poachers' weapon?"

"That's correct."

"I can show you exactly where the sheep fell on my topographical map."

Andrew motioned for the rangers to follow him into the cabin. He unrolled his map on the table and, using a pen, pointed to the spot where the sheep were when they fell and the ridge where he had spotted the poachers.

Bob asked, "What's this mark here?" Pointing to the rune symbol Andrew had marked on the map.

"That's about where I set up my tent."

"I think there's something in your story about this hike that you are not telling us."

"I've told you everything I can think of that will help you catch the poachers."

"We've been trying to catch what we think is an organized ring of poachers who've been stealing big game heads for a while now. This is a sensitive mission. We hope you'll refrain from giving out any of these details. There's a lot of money involved here and these guys can be ruthless. If they knew you were a possible witness, you could be in serious danger."

"I don't think there's any way they could've seen me. What about Jane? Is she in danger?'

"If the poachers think she can identify them, or if they know she's connected to Bill Rutherfield, she could be in trouble. That's why we're trying to report this as a simple horse stealing incident. We're hoping that no one will believe Jane thinks she was attacked by poachers.

"By providing us with a good location of the fresh sheep carcasses, you've saved us a lot of time searching. In the past, we've only found long dead animals with missing heads as evidence. Also, we'll send a crew up to the ridge where the poachers were shooting from. If they were careless or cocky, we might find a shell casing."

They shook hands all around.

"Thank you very much. Whatever training you've had, or whatever you did at TT&T has made you an above average witness. If you can think of anything else, please contact us. Here's my card."

"I hope you get these guys."

After the rangers left, Andrew sat and reviewed the whole experience. He decided there was nothing he could add to what he'd told the rangers. He hoped that they were not too suspicious about why he had chosen to explore the Lulu City area.

He picked up the brochure about the Shipler House Museum and looked it over. It looked like an interesting place. While checking out one of the ranch bicycles, Marge caught him as he was putting the bike tag in his cabin pigeon hole.

"There's our local hero."

"Not really. I just happened to come along at the right time. Anyone would have done the same."

"From the way Jane blushed when I forced her to tell the details, I doubt that anyone would have done the same. We know about you and Jane on the train."

"I guess it's impossible to keep a secret in a small town. Do you have a lot of horse thieves around here?"

"Not since the last one was hanged... joking. Most of the folks who come to the high country are nature lovers, so we don't have much trouble. It's considered a crime wave if some tourist kid steals candy from the country store."

"I'm going to take a bike ride to Grand Lake and check out the Shipler House."

"When you get there ask for Luke and tell him that Marge sent you. He'll give you the 50 cent tour. Nobody knows more about the history of this area than Luke."

"Thanks, Marge."

The Shipler House was an old two story log cabin with a fairly new one story extension on one end. Andrew found a volunteer receptionist and told her Marge from Elk Park Ranch said he should ask for Luke.

"I think he's back in the shop fixing something or other. Go through the door, down the hall to the right, and out the door."

Andrew went down the hall and found a door marked 'employees only'. He tried the door, found it unlocked, and went through to a room full of a mixture of old furniture, shelves full of miscellaneous artifacts, and an older bearded man working at a bench.

"Howdy son, what can I do for you?"

"My name is Andrew Olofsson. Marge up at Elk Park Ranch told me you might give me a history lesson about the area."

"If you're staying at Marge's place, you are probably the fellow who saved Jane from the horse thief."

"Does this town have some kind of telegraph that sends notes to everyone? Or maybe your phones are still using party lines everyone listens on."

"Well, son, If you want to be anonymous, you don't want to hang around these parts."

"Yeah. I'm learning that."

"Olofsson, huh, with a double s?"

Andrew nodded.

"Sounds Swedish. We've not had many Swedes around here lately. Back in the old days, when folks were hoping to strike it rich prospecting, there were a couple of Swedes that came through. Had a few more Germans though."

"You mean like the Germans they kicked out of Lulu City?"

"Hmm…" Luke paused and gave Andrew a long steady look. Andrew returned the gaze. Luke finally broke the silence.

"It seems to me, young fellow, that for a stranger, you already know quite a bit about our history."

"Only what I've been able to read about, and there's not much to be read. There's especially precious little about Lulu City that I can find in print."

"So it's Lulu City you're interested in' huh? Now that's something to ponder on."

Luke gave Andrew another long look.

Andrew realized that in spite of his appearance, Luke was not simply a local 'character' or county bumpkin. He had the kind of eyes that look right into you, and made you feel like you were the emperor with no clothes.

Luke said, "If it's special kind of history you want, it's going to cost you."

"OK, Luke, point me to your favorite watering hole, and I'll stand you for a drink or two."

"Andrew, my boy, it looks like you not only know a little about the history around here, but you know how to pay off your informants. Let me tell the clerk of the day where I'm going."

Andrew followed Luke down the street to the Marmot Tavern. After Luke greeted the regulars and nodded to the bartender, they settled into what was apparently Luke's favorite booth. The bartender came over, put a bottle of Coors and a beer mug down in front of Luke, and asked Andrew what he wanted to drink.

"I'll have one of those." Andrew replied, pointing to Luke's beer.

Luke smiled and said, "Son, it looks like you and me can probably be friends. And that's not just because you helped Jane out of a jam. You don't act like most of the flat landers that come through here. What's your game? And don't give me that phony nature photographer story you've been spreading."

For some reason, there was something in Luke's stare that seemed to look right into him and made Andrew want to spill it all.

"I'm hoping that this will not go out on the Grand Lake party line right away, but here goes."

Andrew then told the story about Arvid, beginning with Aunt Annie's story of how Arvid had come from Sweden, and how he was a dreamer. Even though he could have used his skills as a blacksmith and boat builder, he refused to settle into a job like his brother. Instead, Arvid had wandered off to Colorado, and the only thing to show for it was a little tin box with it's silver ingot and map, and a promise of riches.

Andrew told Luke about TT&T closing down and that he was out of a job, but had little interest in finding another one like it.

They went through another round of beers. Luke quietly listened to Andrew talk and offered no comments. He simply maintained that penetrating stare that kept Andrew going.

Andrew told Luke that he didn't really expect to find any valuable treasure Arvid might have hidden away; he didn't need more money. He explained how he felt guilty about being financially sound only because his parents had been killed in an accident and that he had inherited their estate, something he did not think he deserved. He told him how Aunt Annie kept pushing on him to get beyond being an overgrown college student and get out and have some adventures while he was still young.

These were things he had never told anyone before. There was no one in his life that he could open up to like this. Why he had this sudden urge to unload on this unlikely stranger he didn't know. There was just something in Luke's gaze that kept him talking

Finally, Luke spoke. Luke didn't say, "There there, have another beer," or "it must have been hard losing your folks like that," or "it's OK, there are better days ahead," or anything that most people might have said. The feeling Luke projected with those quiet eyes said it all without the need to speak.

Instead he said, "In our little museum, we have a lot of things that have appeared over the years that no one seems to know what to do with. Someone dies and the family has to empty old closets, and boxes, and trunks, and drawers, that have not seen light for many years. Sometimes they discover some old pictures and have no idea who is in them. There are odd knickknacks that no one in the family wants. Instead of throwing the stuff in the trash, they throw it at us.

"We have old letters, post cards, and newspapers. We also get books. Not novels or great classic literature, although we do get some of those. We sometimes get old business books with records of purchases that were made, items that were sold, and how much was paid to whom for what. Not all of the people who came to the mining towns were ignorant no-skill prospectors chasing fools gold. Some of them were smart entrepreneurs who could read, write, cipher, and operate a successful business. They followed the boom towns, and if the boom went bust, they simply moved on.

"Now, you mentioned that this Uncle Arvid, when he was in Sweden, did some blacksmith work. It just so happens that I seem to remember that one of the business books in our collection is from a Lulu City blacksmith. Let's go back to the museum and see if we can find it. You never know about these things."

After accidentally discovering Arvid's grave because of an unpredictable train accident, and finding Jane, loosing Jane, and then finding her again, Andrew was starting to think that some mysterious forces were directing his life. Maybe here was another coincidence waiting to be revealed.

Back at the museum, Luke started digging through a pile of dusty old books. Finally he came out of the pile holding a book with Lulu City Schmied on the cover. Luke explained that Schmied is German for blacksmith. On the first inside page was written Klaus Schmidt. One inside section had a record of purchases; still another section was a record of customers. Another section had a list of payments made to employees. There was a line: *Arvid Jonsson, May 1880, $4.00*. This was repeated a number of times with different amounts. The last notation was from 1881.

Luke said, "By golly, we found him. Now you can be sure that Arvid was in Lulu City, and he managed to pay his way by working for Herr Schmidt."

"Thank you very much, Luke. Now I know Uncle Arvid was not simply a dreamer. He had his dreams, but he clearly was willing to work hard while chasing his dreams."

"My guess is that Arvid must have made the silver ingot you found in the tin box. He certainly had the metal working skills to do so. It's not very likely, however, that he discovered any rich deposit of silver. The ore found around Lulu City was never valuable enough to make it worth while to haul to a mill for processing, and there were never enough investors to finance building a local mill.

"There was, however, a lot of money to be made by selling shares in claims. Guys would high grade an assay. They would gather a sample of ore from a claim and process it down until an assay would report the sample was worth many dollars per ton. Sometimes the assayers were even in on the scam. The claim holders would take a copy of the assay to investors with the promise that with an investment, mills would be built, workers would be hired, shafts drilled, and the investors would become rich. For a good description of this, read Mark Twain's book Roughing It."

Andrew thought about the papers in Arvid's tin box. Perhaps Arvid was returning to the east to line up investors in a silver mine, and that was how the family was going get rich. He would probably never know. However, he still wanted to return to the location of the rune mark on Arvid's map to see if he could find anything. That mark had to mean something.

"Thank you, Luke. You've filled in another piece of the Arvid puzzle. But more than that, thanks for being such a good listener. I think your allowing me to ramble on has helped me clear out some old cobwebs that have been clouding my brain."

Luke gave Andrew a firm handshake, "I'm very happy you came by. I think before your Colorado adventure is over you might just find out who you really are."

Andrew got on the bike and headed back to the ranch.

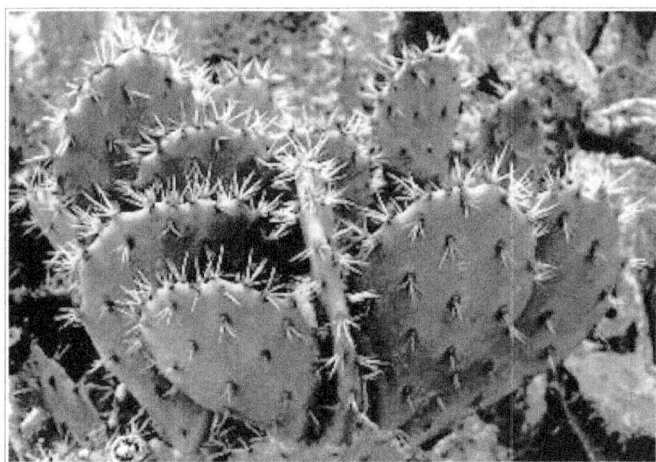

## Chapter 15 - Andrew Gets the Point.

After his visit with Luke at the museum, Andrew decided to stop at the Grand Lake Dairy King for lunch. He ordered a mushroom burger with fries and a chocolate shake. When he went to pay, the girl at the cash register said, "Just a minute, please," disappeared, and a minute later came back with the manager.

"You're Andrew, aren't you?"

"Yes, I have to confess, I'm Andrew."

"Well, this is on the house. Jane is one of our favorite people. And we want to thank you for saving her life."

The employees came out and gave Andrew a round of applause.

"Look," Andrew said, "This is silly. I just did what I'm sure any of you would have done."

"Honey, you're now a local hero, and we need all of those we can get."

Andrew sighed and bit his tongue. He found this embarrassing and wondered how long it would continue.

When he got back to the ranch and went in to return the bike lock key to the keyboard, Marge was on duty at the desk.

"Here's our local hero."

"Look Marge, I wish you'd put a stop to this hero thing. I'm finding it embarrassing. I'm just not comfortable with the attention. I was just at the Dairy King, and they didn't charge me for my lunch, and the staff all came out and applauded. It makes me want to hide somewhere."

"I'm sorry, Andrew. Maybe things have gotten a little out of hand."

"Can you maybe get on your Grand Lake party line, or however gossip is spread around here, and quiet this down a little?"

"I'll see what I can do. Did you enjoy your mushroom burger and shake?"

"Arrgh! I give up."

"Andrew, it's hard to remain a stranger in a small town. It's much better to have a reputation as a good guy than as the town bum. Did you know that they found Jane's horse?"

"No. Where did they find it?"

"It was tied to a tree in the woods behind the general store. Ned went over with the horse trailer and is taking it to the barn."

"Thanks for the info."

Andrew immediately went to the barn where he found Ned leading the horse to a stall.

"Hey Ned, I see the horse is back."

"Yep. A town kid found it and I just got back from picking her up."

"Has anyone touched the saddle or anything?"

"Not yet, I was just getting ready to brush her down and feed her. She's had a rough couple of days."

Andrew handed Ned the card the ranger had given him at the interview.

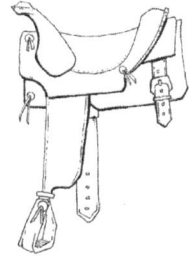

"Here's the number for the ranger who's investigating the incident. Maybe we should give him a call. There might be some useful evidence… fingerprints or something, that would help with the investigation.

"That's a good idea. I'll call him right away."

Ned went to the office in the corner of the barn and made the call while Andrew waited.

When Ned hung up he reported, "The ranger said he would contact the state patrol and they would send a crime scene tech out. The NPS doesn't have any crime lab of their own, so they use the staties when they need this kind of work done. I'll make sure no one touches anything on the saddle until they do their thing."

"Thanks, Ned. It might be a long shot, but we need to do everything we can to get the guy who attacked Jane."

Andrew headed back to his cabin. Passing the swimming pool, he noticed Jane was there doing some cleaning. As he approached the pool, she suddenly disappeared under the water. It seemed she was under for a very long time, and Andrew started getting worried. He rushed over to the side of the pool and was ready to jump in when she popped up out of the water, shook her head, and a spray of water twinkled in the sunshine. She spotted Andrew.

"Hey Andrew. You caught me trying to clear a clogged drain."

"You were under so long I thought I should jump in and rescue you."

"Ah! Trying to be a hero again! Your reputation in town is already established; you don't really have to embellish it by rescuing women who may or may not really need rescuing."

"Don't tell me about this hero nonsense. I've already been embarrassed enough."

"Not used to small town gossip spreading, are you?"

"No, and I hate being called a hero, and I hate the unwanted attention. What were you doing, disappearing under the water like that?"

"I'm trying to clear a clogged drain. You'd be amazed at what people throw into pools."

Jane took a deep breath and disappeared again. Andrew started to be concerned about how long she was under, but finally, she popped up with a water shedding toss of her head.

"You won't believe what was clogging the drain this time."

She waved a piece of cloth at Andrew; it took a minute before he recognized a bikini top. She laughed,"Here's something for your pervert club collection."

"The only bikini top I've seen lately is the one some sexy sunbather almost lost the other day."

Jane hauled back and threw it at Andrew. It flew high and wide of the mark, and Andrew stepped back and reached out to make the catch. When he stepped back, his foot landed on a rubber duck that had been left on the pool apron. He lost his balance and fell, his back and side brushing against a cactus that was part of the pool landscaping.

"Andrew, are you OK?"

"I would be better if I wasn't a human pincushion."

As Andrew got up he groaned and it was obvious he was in pain. Jane climbed out of the pool and rushed to his side."

"Let me take a look. Oh my, you have quite a collection of cactus spines on your side; we have to get them out. Come on to my cabin. I've got tweezers and a first aid kit."

Jane hurried toward her cabin; Andrew followed along. He limped a little, trying to keep thorns that were stuck in his shirt and pants from digging into his skin. Jane got out her first aid kit.

"Let me take a closer look. You have cactus thorns on your side, down your leg, and on your butt. Some of those thorns are too big for tweezers."

She went to a cabinet drawer and found some needle nose pliers.

"Take off your shirt. Stand here at the end of the bed, and drop your pants. Then lay face down on the bed so I can do a little operation."

Andrew unbuttoned his shirt and gently pulled it away from his side. Fortunately, his shoes had a loose fit. He managed to kick them off by using the heel of one foot to shove the shoe off the other.

He carefully removed his pants and stretched out on the bed.

"Is this your revenge for my catching you naked on the train, and peeking at your slipped bikini when you were tied up?"

Jane smiled, "Don't forget, we've been naked together more than once. This should be old stuff by now. Crap, I'm dripping all over the floor. I have to get out of this wet suit."

She slipped out of the swimsuit, tossed it over a chair, and grabbed a shirt.

"Seeing you naked is always a pleasure. Ouch!"

Jane carefully started removing cactus thorns. The bigger ones required the pliers, while tweezers worked for the smaller ones. Andrew alternated between flinching with pain each time a thorn was removed, and feeling ecstatic at the touch of Jane's fingers on his skin.

Jane found a tube of antiseptic cream in the first aid kit, sat on the bed next to Andrew, and gently rubbed the cream over the area where the thorns had been. Andrew had to shift his position a little to ease the growing pressure he was feeling. He glanced at Jane and noticed that her face was flushed, and the flush extended to her neck and chest. They quietly savored the feelings for a moment until Jane finally broke the spell. In a somewhat husky voice, she said, "I think that should prevent any infection from the thorn pricks."

"Maybe I should come back tonight and you could rub some more cream on, just in case."

"In your dreams, cactus boy."

"A boy's got to have a dream."

"Before you put your clothes back on, you better check to make sure there are no thorns stuck in the fabric."

Jane got dressed and put the first aid kit away.

"Thanks much for the treatment, nurse Jane. It'll be a long time before I forget this experience. Can I take you out for dinner this evening as a thank you?"

"OK. There's no Leone's in Grand Lake, but there's a popular Mexican place over in Granby. Why don't you meet me in front of the office around six?"

"It's a date. See you then."

Later, Andrew found Jane waiting in her jeep in front of the office.

"Nice wheels for a poor former grad student."

"I never thought I would ever be able to afford something like this."

Jane told Andrew the story of the mid-eastern student who had to go home and sold her the jeep, cheap.

Then she frowned and said, "I'm not sure why I'm telling you this, but you already know about my deal with Uncle Bill. The story about how I got the jeep is a lie. This jeep belonged to Uncle Bill. He wasn't using it much anymore, and he knew I needed transportation, so he was going to loan it to me. I told him, I wasn't comfortable driving around in a borrowed vehicle, so he sold it to me for a price I couldn't refuse. Bill and I made up the cover story to minimize local knowledge about our connection."

"I see. The way gossip flies around town, you figured if people guessed you were working with Bill, the word might get to the bad guys. Don't worry, I'll faithfully believe this jeep used to be owned by a mysterious student from the mid east."

At Casa Granby, Andrew got a quick introduction to real Mexican food. Real Mexican food was not something found in Madison, New Jersey. Jane suggested the combination plate that included a taco, a chicken enchilada, rice, beans, and lettuce all sprinkled with cheese. For dessert, they had Sopapillas, hollow triangles of deep fried dough they filled with honey.

"You can't find anything like this in Madison, New Jersey. I'm going to have to do some serious hiking to counteract the feast I've just pigged out on," sighed Andrew."

"I have to work again tomorrow." Jane remembered, "Maybe Wednesday you could go with me for a visit to an old Basque sheepherder. I promised Uncle Bill I would ask him if he had noticed any usual hunting activity."

"I'm in. Where do we find this sheepherder?"

"He runs a small herd in the hills over toward Hot Sulphur Springs."

"Visiting with a Basque sheepherder sounds interesting. It'll make a nice addition to my education about life in the high country."

Arvid's Treasure

## Chapter 16 - The Green Mountain Hike

Andrew decided he needed to avoid Lulu City for a while and instead work on his nature photographer cover story. He studied the guide book and found that the Green Mountain trail would be a good place to start a hike. It would also burn off some of the big Mexican meal.

At the breakfast buffet he found Jane, Nancy, and Ned having breakfast together. They motioned to Andrew to join them, and Ned asked Andrew if he had any hikes planned.

"As a matter of fact I do. I've been looking at the trail map brochures in the rack in the office, and I think I'll take the Green Mountain trail up to the Big Meadows. I understand the meadows is a good spot to see some big game."

Ned said, "Some Moose hang out around the meadows; there are marshy places they like. You'll have a pretty good chance of seeing some elk, and there are nearly always mule deer around."

"Are you doing a day loop, or some back country camping?" asked Jane.

"I think I'll spend a couple of nights out."

Nancy jumped into the conversation.

"If you want to spend the time, you might go on up to Granite Falls. The scenery up there is great, and there are some nice back country camping sites."

"Thanks for the suggestion."

The group then spent some time trying to educate him about hiking in the mountains. Ted told him that going up 1,000 feet at the same latitude had the same affect on the climate as going 500 miles north at the same elevation. Jane reminded him how fast the temperature in the high country can change from sunbathing weather at 80 degrees to a snowstorm. Nancy told him to be sure he had clothes that could be used in layers.

Ned said there were not as many bears on the west side of the park as there were on the east side, but a bear could surprise him. If he saw one, he should make a lot of noise because bears didn't like to be around humans. Ned also reminded him to keep food in animal proof containers. The group continued to suggest other things they thought a flat lander needed to know about hiking in the mountains. Andrew thanked them all for the suggestions, and went back to his cabin.

Andrew loaded his back pack with his Nikon, water, a supply of trail mix, freeze dried meals, a couple of energy bars, a light weight stove for heating water, a water filter for refilling his water bottle, and set off. The trail started at just under 9,000 feet in elevation. Some of the trails connected to the Green Mountain trail had elevation gains of over 3,000 feet.

At the trail head parking lot, two couples were loading up their cars.

"Just coming off the trail?" Andrew asked.

"We've been up there three days. It's a wonderful area for hiking and camping."

"When you started your hike, did you see any other hikers, or anything unusual?"

"No, there was no one else on the trails where we hiked."

Another one of the hikers asked, "What do you mean unusual?"

"A couple of days ago a woman had her horse stolen just up the valley from here, and the park rangers are trying to identify the thief."

"There was a big black pickup truck here when we arrived. Remember Lou, you said it was an unusual vehicle for backpackers. Most hikers don't drive big crew cab pickups."

Andrew thought this was interesting, and asked, "By any chance were you taking pictures when you were getting ready to start your hike?"

Andrew guessed most hiking groups probably took a lot of pictures to remember their adventures, and show to their families.

"This is a trip to celebrate Lou's 30th birthday. We probably have been taking more pictures than Japanese tourists."

"It would be good if you could stop at the Kawuneeche Visitor Center on your way by, and tell Ranger Joe or Bob what you saw. You might have a clue that could help catch a horse thief."

"We were planning to stop there anyway. After days on the trail, it's nice to find a real toilet and hot water."

Andrew hoped the information about the pickup truck might turn out to be useful. He said goodbye to the hikers, and headed on up the trail. He spent the next two days exploring the trails around Green Mountain.

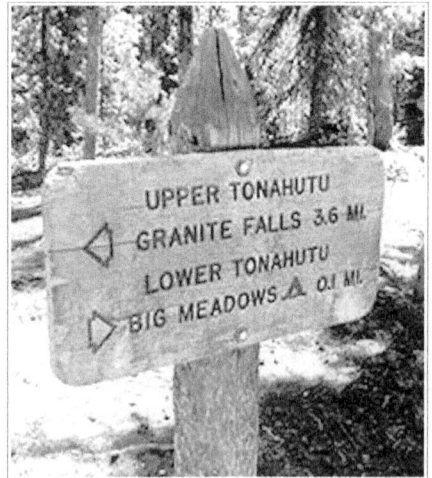

He tried to remember the lessons he learned from Tom Brown; rather then just stomping along the trails, he moved slowly, hoping that he would be less likely to frighten off the wildlife and that he could take some good pictures. Tom Brown had taught to use shotgun or spatter vision rather than tunnel vision, and to always look for subtle changes in colors or unnatural shapes.

Since he didn't have any special photo assignment to worry about, Andrew didn't just search for big game. Nothing was off his list. He managed to get some good shots of mule deer, and hoped his moose pictures might be good.

He quickly learned was it was easier to get a decent picture of a mule deer or moose, then it was to capture a chickadee or Steller's Jay. Birds just don't stay in one place long enough to focus on them. Wildflowers were another problem. They didn't flit around like chickadees, but the slightest breeze kept them moving in and out of focus.

Landscape pictures were probably the easiest to capture. The snow covered peaks were wonderful, and catching their reflections in a mountain lake was worth the effort. Andrew observed that the lighting of scenes changed dramatically from morning to evening, and changes in lighting caused by the clouds moving across the scene could make a difference between an ordinary snapshot, and a gallery quality photograph.

All in all, Andrew found that the two days in the mountains seemed to soothe his soul, and made him lose the anxiety he had felt since the closing of TT&T.

## Chapter 17 - The Newspaper Man

The morning after Andrew returned from his Green Mountain hike, he headed over to the breakfast buffet. As he passed the office, Marge stopped him and suggested he look in his pigeon hole because he had a message. The message was from Amos Shipler and read, "Please call me when you get back from your hike."

"Who is Amos Shipler?"Andrew asked Marge.

"He runs the *Grand Lake Spectator*, our area newspaper. I think he probably wants to interview you."

"Does he have any connection to the Shipler House Museum that I visited?"

"He's actually descended from the man who built the Shipler House. His family goes way back in the history of this area."

"I'll call him after breakfast. I just hope that it's not more of the hero nonsense."

Andrew filled his plate from the breakfast bar and once again joined Jane, Nancy, and Ned. They asked about his hike, and he gave them a thumbnail sketch of where he went, what he saw, and answered their questions about the hike.

"Did you get any good pictures?" Jane asked with a conspiratorial wink.

"I burned through three 36 exposure rolls of film. I won't know if I got anything worth showing until after they've been developed. I'm using Agfa film and I buy it with prepaid mailers. All I have to do is pop the envelopes in the mail and wait for the pictures to come back."

Ned asked if he was shooting slide or negative film.

"I mostly use color negative film. Agfa sends me back a package with both prints and a set of negatives.

"By the way, there was a message in my pigeon hole to call Amos Shipler. Do you guys know anything about him?"

Ted said, "He runs the local newspaper and has his fingers in a lot of things around here. His family was very important in the early days of the area, and he has a lot of influence in these parts."

"Amos probably knows more about what goes on around here than anybody," Nancy added.

"Well, I guess I'd better give him a call. Maybe he wants to ask me about the horse thief incident."

Jane asked him what his plans were for the day.

"Well, I have to talk to this Shipler fellow. How about you take me back to the Casa Granby for dinner tonight?"

Nancy chimed in, "Oh Ho! I think you two have got something going on here."

Jane poked her on the arm, "Shut up, Nancy."

"After I get this visit to Amos Shipler out of the way, I thought I'd check out the local library."

Nancy rubbed her arm where Jane had poked her.

"You might be surprised when you see our library; it's a lot more than you would expect for such a small town. It's been in operation since the 1800's and got a real boost in the early 1900's after the Moffat Tunnel was built. Once the trains came through, it was much easier for people to get here from Denver."

Jane interrupted, "There was some sort of scandal about funding for the tunnel. It seems that some of the Denver big wigs owned property around Winter Park and wanted to build a resort there. By coincidence, Winter Park is right at the western end of the tunnel."

"That's true," Nancy continued. "Even back in the early 1900's there were a lot of people who enjoyed excursions to the mountains. You can find a

lot of old photos of both men and women who found their way to Rocky Mountain National Park.

"When the train came through, it was easier for people, at least people with money, to visit the west side of the park than the east side."

Ned added, "The best way to get to the east side of the park was to ride up the steep road in a Stanley Steamer. As a matter of fact, the early patrons of the Stanley Hotel in Estes Park got there in Mr. Stanley's famous steam powered car."

Nancy continued, "As a result of the train access, Grand Lake got a lot of rich visitors, and some of them supported the local library. So, our local library has a long history."

"OK, you convinced me to visit the library."

After breakfast was over, Andrew made his call to Amos Shipler.

"Hello, this is Andrew Olofsson. I got your message for me to call."

"Yes, thanks for calling me back. I'd like to visit with you. How about having lunch with me at the Marmot Tavern where you had drinks with Luke the other day?"

Andrew thought to himself, it sure is hard to have secrets around here.

"All right. What time should I be there?"

"Let's get a head start, say around 11:30?"

"OK, see you there."

Andrew went back to his cabin and read for a while until it was time to meet with Amos. At the Marmot Tavern, Andrew asked the bartender if Amos Shipler was there. The bartender replied that he hadn't arrived yet, so Andrew took a seat in the same booth he and Luke had occupied a couple of days earlier.

A well dressed distinguished looking man entered the Tavern, shook hands and greeted everyone as he made his way to Andrew's booth. As he approached the booth, Andrew stood up.

"You're the famous Andrew Olofsson, I presume."

"And I presume that you're the famous Amos Shipler." Andrew replied.

Amos gave Andrew a firm handshake as they sat down.

"It's an honor to meet you. I've heard you are a major personality here in Grand Lake," Andrew said.

"Please, let's not be so formal. From what Silas Redfern told me about you, I doubt that you used to talk to your old boss so formally."

"How do you know Silas Redfern was my boss?"

"I'm a newspaper man; information is my business. I have my sources. If I don't, I usually can find someone who does. Let's order, then we can have a little talk."

When the bartender came for their order, Andrew decided to try a Philly cheese steak sandwich, french fries and a Coors beer. Amos ordered a rib eye steak, with a baked potato. He asked Andrew, "Would you rather have a glass of Zinfandel instead of the beer?"

"I might if this was dinner, but I think I'll stick with beer. What's your source for knowing about Silas Redfern."

"You might be surprised that we have a very good library here."

"Actually, I've heard something about it."

"The library has a modest collection of periodicals. Because we get a lot of folks through here who are interested in hiking and the outdoors, TT&T is included in the collection; perhaps I should say, was included. I was sorry to learn that it's been discontinued.

"I went through the back issues on file. I must say that I'm impressed with your contributions to the magazine."

"Thank you. I enjoyed the job while it lasted. Silas Redfern was about as good a boss as could be found anywhere."

"He also had very good things to say about you. I also talked with Luke about your meeting with him. Of course, Luke would never discuss the details of conversations. He did say, however, that he was favorably impressed by you; and that says a lot because Luke does not impress easily. He has a penetrating stare that frightens people, or puts them off. So, I'm pleased that the two of you hit it off so well."

"That's nice of you to say, but I'm still not sure why you called this meeting."

"How do you like this part of Colorado so far?"

"I have to admit that I like what I've seen so far. But I've only been here a short time, not enough time to develop a strong opinion one way or another. I think I'd have to spend at least a full year, go through all of the seasons, and learn a lot more about the area before I could decide how much I like it."

"You're not impulsive. You seem to be careful before jumping into things. That's a good thing."

"Again, I have to ask; why am I here? When I got your message and found out you were with the local newspaper, I assumed you were going to ask me about the horse thief incident."

"I probably know more about the horse stealing incident than you can guess. I told you that I have sources, and my sources work both ways. They inform me of things because they know I won't publicize things that are better kept private. They also know I'll keep them in the loop when I learn of things they need to know. This is not like some towns or cities where the press and the law enforcement agencies act like adversaries. We're too small for that.

"I'm sure you've noticed that gossip travels very fast here. But that doesn't mean everyone knows everything. When it comes to accurate news reporting, or effective law enforcement, we know when to keep things out of the gossip channels.

"In the case of the horse stealing, I can tell you there are things going on that are a lot bigger than taking a horse. And, I know you know that also. And you've demonstrated you can keep quiet when it's better to keep quiet.

"The reason I went to the trouble to contact your former boss is that I wanted to know about your personal abilities and integrity."

"Why is that so important?"

"I know that you're currently between jobs. Have you made up your mind what to do next with your career?"

"I have to admit that's a question I'm still struggling with."

"Here it is then. I'm not asking for any quick decision, but I'm looking for someone to help run my newspaper. I'm not getting any younger, and I have to look ahead. I've read every article you've ever published in TT&T. There's no one locally who has the writing skills you have. You don't have newspaper experience, but that just takes a little time and effort to acquire. I want you to seriously look at my paper and see if you can imagine yourself as part of my team."

Andrew exclaimed, "Wow! That's a big surprise. I'm going to have to do a lot of research and soul searching before I can even start to try imagining what you're suggesting."

"Good enough. We'll leave it there. You keep chasing around and see if you can find yourself. Let's keep in touch."

"Thank you. I think you've just given me one of the best compliments I've ever received. Now, can I pay for our lunch?"

"Don't be silly. Just get on your bike and go back to the ranch. And when those bike wheels start turning, I hope the wheels in your brain will also start turning."

"My mind is already spinning."

With that, Andrew and Amos shook hands and Andrew headed for the library. He still had time before he met Jane for dinner.

## Chapter 18 - Bill Works the Case

Bill Rutherfield made a call to his contacts at the RMNP Timber Creek Ranger Station. He explained the situation to Bob, and suggested that he arrange to interview Jane and this Andrew guy. He also asked Bob to get a crew together to try and locate the sheep carcasses. He told Bob that Jane said the Andrew guy might be able to locate the spot where the incident took place on a topographical map.

With two new fresh big horn heads on their hands, Bill knew the poachers would have to get them to a taxidermist soon. Earlier in the poaching investigation, he had identified all of the taxidermists in Colorado, Wyoming, Oklahoma, New Mexico, and Texas.

He faxed a memo to wildlife officers to monitor any questionable activities in or around these businesses. Most taxidermists were also hunters who supported good sportsmanship; however, there were a few lone wolf taxidermists worth watching.

The fax caught the attention of Max Smith, a game warden who worked out of the Alamosa, Colorado, office. He had been suspicious of Rob

Role's operation in Manassa, but he'd never been able to prove anything illegal.

Manassa was a small town with a population of less than 1,000. It's major claim to fame was that one time heavyweight champion boxer Jack Dempsey was born there. Dempsey was known as The Manassa Mauler. Manassa is also known as a source of gem quality turquoise.

It was not possible for an outsider to run a stakeout in Manassa without being observed and alerting everyone in the town. However, the Mormons had a small church there, and Max Smith had quite a few Mormon friends. He made contact, and asked if they could check around to see if anyone had noticed any unusual activity around the Role place.

Several hours later, Max got a call. A dog walker had seen a newer big black SUV pull up to Role's shop. It was there a very short time since by the time the dog walker had made his circuit around the block, the SUV was gone. Max faxed this information back to Bill.

The rangers who had interviewed Andrew were armed with excellent information as to the location of the sheep kill. Andrew's film was processed and several frames were enlarged to 16 by 20 prints. The NPS team located the kill and removed two sheep carcasses to Denver for analysis. Two bullets were found in the carcasses. One had hit a bone and was badly mangled. The other remained intact.

The team had also, with the help of Andrew's map, found the place where the poacher had made his shot. They scanned the area using a metal detector and found a cartridge. The bullet and cartridge were sent to the State Police forensic lab for analysis. Ballistics tests yielded rifling, characteristic marks on one of the bullets, and the analysis of the shell casing determined that the weapon used was a Blaser R93. The ballistics analysis and the information that the weapon used was a Blaser R93 were sent to the FBI and ATF.

A state patrol trooper came to the ranch to collect the saddle from Jane's horse. Before the saddle was loaded up for sending to the Crime Lab in Denver, they asked Jane to inspect the bag with her clothes and things. She was surprised that everything in the bag seemed to be undisturbed. The bag with her things was fabric and did not offer any chance of finding finger prints, so Jane was allowed to keep it.

Jane and Ned were asked to provide finger prints for comparison with any prints found on the saddle. Analysis at the lab found several usable prints that didn't match Jane's or Ned's; the prints found were from two different individuals.

While Bill was doing research and gathering evidence to catch the poachers, Tex Frey was doing his own research. He once again called Dante's Bar in Frisco, Colorado, and asked Vinnie to get word to Butch to give him a call.

It was the next day before Butch called Tex.

"What's up, boss? You got another hunting job already?"

"No. We have some details to clean up from the last job. I've been wondering about how that girl got loose. Are you sure she was tied up tight?"

"Yeah. There's no way she could have untied herself. I jumped on her back and tied her hands with a pigging string almost before she was awake. I pulled the ski mask backwards over her head so she wouldn't be able to see anything. Then I cut strips from that saddle blanket she was laying on, and retied her hands so I could take my pigging string back. I tied her feet with a blanket strip, and used another to hog tie her. That saddle blanket material is tough. There's no way she could have broken loose."

"Well' she sure disappeared, didn't she? Are you absolutely sure that when we went to look for her we were looking in the right place?"

"I'm sure about that. And remember, we not only looked at where I was sure I left her, but we searched all around the area."

"Well, that leaves only one possibility. Someone must have untied her. That means there must have been another witness."

"But we would have seen them. The only way for them to get out of there would have been to follow the same trail we used to get back to the truck."

"I don't know about that. I'm convinced we might have a problem with two witnesses. You need to get back over there and find out what happened to that girl. And you need to do it soon, you understand?"

"I understand, boss. I'll get on it."

# Arvid's Treasure

## Chapter 19 - The Sheep and the Sand Dune Pony

Jane had put in enough hours of work to fulfill the obligation of her part-time job at the ranch for the week. She thought about calling Uncle Bill and asking him how his investigation was going. On second thought, she decided, it was probably a bad idea. First of all, he probably couldn't discuss the case with her or anyone else not officially involved. Secondly, she would only give him an opportunity to play Dutch Uncle again and burn her ears about what he considered her reckless behavior. She was certainly not ready to answer questions about her relationship with Andrew. She was not even able to answer questions to herself about that.

She had, however, promised Uncle Bill to pay a visit to Mikel, the sheepherder. This required a trip into the mountains to Mikel's sheep camp. She decided to ask Andrew if he would like to ride along. They met again at the breakfast buffet.

"How did your interview with Aron Shipler go?"

"It wasn't anything I expected." Andrew replied. "I thought he was probably doing a story about the horse thief incident, but he never brought that up.

He's a very interesting guy. He'd taken a lot of trouble to check out my background. For example, he said that he'd read my articles in back issues of TT&T."

"Amos has a reputation of knowing everything about everyone. As far as I know, he's never used what he knows to publish negative stories about anyone. For someone with as much local power and influence as people around here believe he has, I've never heard of anyone claiming he abuses his power.

I'm still planning the excursion to visit an old Basque sheepherder. Are you still willing to go along?"

"Since I feel I'm on some sort of vacation with no schedule or responsibilities, I think I would like that."

"OK, Can you meet me at the jeep in half an hour?"

"Sure, what should I bring?"

"Nothing special. We'll stop at the general store and pick up something to have for lunch. I also want to get a bag of oranges for Mikel. He spends long periods of time alone with his sheep and dogs, so he appreciates getting fresh fruit now and then."

After a brief stop at the general store, they headed down Route 34 and turned west on US 40. Route 40 followed the Colorado River which at this point was no longer the little stream of the Kawuneeche Valley. At one point, the highway dipped down and then up out of a place where there was a dry stream bed crossing the road. Andrew noticed that in the dip, the blacktop pavement changed to concrete, and asked Jane about it.

"There are places where the highway builders decided not to install a culvert or to build a bridge. Instead, they put in these dips to carry water; most of the time these are dry gulches. But when a heavy rain storm hits the area, they can fill up pretty fast. Nowadays, most of the dips have been replaced by bridges, but there are a few of these dips still around."

Andrew recalled, "When I was about 10 years old, Aunt Annie gave me a book called Sand Dune Pony. It was a nice story about a boy and a special pony with big feet good for running in the sand dunes because they didn't sink into the sand. I guess they were kind of like snow shoes.

"Anyway, the thing I remember most about the book is the description of a desert flash flood. In the story, a dry gulch suddenly had a flash flood, even though it had never rained."

"I know that book. The story takes place in southern Colorado at a place that's now Great Sand Dunes National Park. Flash floods happen a lot in the mountains; they don't call these the rocky mountains for no reason. There is very little top soil, and the rain can't soak in.

"There might be a rain storm in the mountains miles away from a dry gulch, the water collects and roars down the gulch, sometimes several feet high, and carries everything with it. In the past these flash floods have even washed away campers who didn't realize they were camping in a dangerous place."

They left Route 40 and drove first on a county road, and then Jane headed up the side of a mountain following some nearly invisible track.

"I assume you know where you're going."

"Don't worry, I've been to Mikel's sheep camp many times. One summer, back when I was working on my Master's degree, I spent several weeks with him. I was observing the interaction of the sheep with wildlife.

"Actually, Uncle Bill introduced us. I learned quite a bit of the history of sheep herding in Colorado. Mikel is kind of a throwback; nowadays sheep ranchers might own several thousand sheep. They typically divide the sheep into smaller flocks and hire herders to work the different flocks.

"Nearly all of the herders are what is called H-2A workers. H-2A is a special foreign worker program that allows immigrants to stay in the country for certain agricultural jobs; nowadays the sheepherders are mostly from Peru or other South American countries. The ranch owners can't find local workers willing to take what is an isolated, lonely, low paying job. To a peasant from Peru, however, the pay is high; they can work for a few years here and then return home with enough money to build a house and raise a family.

"A hundred years ago most of the sheep herders were Basques, from the border area between Spain and France. They were mostly hard workers able to take advantage of homesteading laws and create a good life for their families. There are still Basque cultural celebrations in a number of towns in the Rockies where they feature costumes, dancing, food and preserve the Basque culture here in the US."

"You said that Mikel was a throwback. What do you mean by that?"

"Mikel has a Basque heritage, but he doesn't work for a large sheep ranching operation or co op. He, along with his dogs, only run a couple of hundred sheep. He'll never get rich, but he is content to live a life style he prefers. He has no boss, is pretty much self-sufficient, and enjoys some of the best scenery anywhere; for him, life is good."

As the jeep crawled up into the mountains, Andrew pointed out what looked like an old covered wagon in the distance.

"That's a traditional sheep wagon. The design goes back maybe a couple of hundred years. It's the equivalent of a modern camping trailer, and has everything needed for a herder to spend several months with his sheep in relative comfort. Sheep wagons follow the herd. On a big sheep ranch, the sheep herds are moved every so often to refresh grazing land. In Mikel's case, his herd is pretty small and he and the dogs can move them around without over grazing any particular spot, so he can keep his wagon in one place for most of the grazing season."

As they approached the sheep wagon, Mikel was there to greet them. When Jane got out of the jeep, Mikel smiled and gave her a hug.

"Jane! When I saw the jeep, I thought Bill was coming to see me."

"This is, or was, Bill's jeep. He sold it to me. This is my friend Andrew. I've been teaching him a little about sheep herding.

"I'm pleased to meet you, Andrew. You've selected a very good, and I have to say, very pretty teacher."

"Yes, I'm lucky It's nice to meet you. Mikel. Jane has been telling me about your idyllic life here in the mountains."

"How have you been, Jane? Are you still involved with your studies?"

"Not really. I have a part-time job at Elk Park Ranch over by Grand Lake. I haven't decided whether to go back to school or not."

"Well, you can always come back up here and become a full time herder." Mikel teased.

"Thanks for the offer. I might consider it if nothing else works out. Here's a bag of oranges we brought you."

"Thank you very much nire neska. You are always worrying about my diet. So what brings you way up here? I doubt that you came all this way just to show your boyfriend a bunch of ragged sheep and a ragged old sheepherder."

"Uncle Bill has been trying to track down a gang of poachers and he wanted me to ask if you've noticed any evidence of them in this area."

"Nothing much lately. I've run across a couple of headless elk carcasses, but nothing recent. I'm afraid

Bill will have to look elsewhere for his poachers. I'll put out the word to some of my sheepherder friends. If I hear anything I'll get word to Bill.

I'm afraid I've forgotten my manners. Can I offer you something to eat?"

"That would be swell."

Mikel warmed up a pot of lamb stew, and they sat and talked for a while. Jane and Mikel reminisced about the days when she was doing her research project.

Mikel talked a little about how the sheep herding business had changed since his great grandfather had come to the mountains, "In the old days, most sheepherders were from Basque country or Greece. Now, they mostly come from Peru. Unlike the Basques who came to stay, the herders from Peru are temporary. They send money home, and they only stay until they have enough to build a house or raise a family back in Peru."

They hiked around for a while and Mikel gave Andrew a demonstration of how his border collies could move sheep around, guided only by a few hand signals and whistles. The afternoon clouds were building up in the northeast, and Jane suggested it was time for them to head back. Mikel made Jane promise to come back sooner next time.

Jane navigated the jeep down the mountain side and back to the highway.

As they approached the dip in the highway, they saw several stopped cars. One of the bystanders told them that a car had been washed off the road, was stuck in the river, and there were people in the car. They looked and saw a woman waving for help from a car stuck in the middle of the river.

Andrew asked Jane, "Is the winch on your jeep working?"

"Yes it is."

"Pull the jeep as close to the river as you can."

"The winch doesn't have enough power to pull that car."

"No, but is has enough power to pull me."

While Jane got the jeep into position, Andrew took off his jacket, threw it into the jeep, and grabbed the winch cable. He wrapped the cable around his waist and clipped the hook to the cable, in effect lassoing himself with the cable. He slowly waded out into the river, dragging the winch cable behind him. The fast moving water nearly swept him off his feet several times, but he made it to the car. He shouted over the roaring river noise to the woman who had been waving from the open window of the car.

"How many people are in the car?"

"Just my daughter Mary and me. Please save Mary."

Mary climbed into her mother's lap.

"Hi Mary. I'm going to give you a ride. Come through the window and put your arms around my neck."

Mary climbed out the car window and put her arms around Andrew's neck. Andrew said to the woman, "When I turn around with my back to you, climb out the window and grab hold of my belt."

Maria, Mary's mother, managed to drag herself through the window. Reaching under the water she felt Andrew's back until she located his belt and hooked both hands around the belt.

"OK, hold on tight and we'll walk back to the shore."

Andrew waved to Jane, who started the winch motor. As the winch motor started winding the cable, Jane heard a collective gasp from the small crowd that had gathered. She looked up and saw that the car had broken loose and was tumbling down the river. Andrew was struggling through the water with a little

232

girl hugging him and a woman following closely behind.

As an EMT truck arrived from the Granby fire station, a woman in a golf cart drove up and parked next to the jeep.

Although it took only a few minutes to fight his way back to the shore, it seemed to Andrew that everything was in slow motion until he reached shallow water. Jane jumped in and took Mary from Andrew's arms. A large man in a fire department uniform stepped out of the crowd, picked Maria up and carried her to the rescue vehicle. Jane handed Mary over to a female EMT crew member. They put Maria on a gurney with Mary next to her, covered them with a space blanket, and sped off to Granby.

Andrew, exhausted, had fallen to his knees in the sand at the edge of the river. Jane went to him, followed closely by the woman from the golf cart.

"Your husband is suffering from hypothermia; we need to get him warmed up. I'm the owner of the Drowsy Creek Lodge. It's just up the hill there. There's a hot tub in cabin #1 where we can warm him up. Get him into your jeep and follow me."

Jane didn't bother to explain to the lady that Andrew wasn't her husband. With the help of a bystander, she managed to get Andrew into the jeep. He was shivering uncontrollably, and his lips were blue. Jane followed the golf cart and parked the jeep in front of the cabin. The golf cart lady was there holding the door open as Jane helped Andrew out of the jeep.

"My name is Martha Pringle and I'm the owner of this place. Get your husband undressed and into the hot tub. You better get out of your wet clothes also. I'm going to rustle up a pot of chicken noodle soup. I'll come back in a couple of minutes and take your clothes to the laundry and dry them out. You'll find robes in the bathroom."

As Jane and Andrew entered the cabin and saw the interior, they looked at each other and they couldn't help laughing. The hot tub was heart shaped, and the room was decorated very much like the honeymoon suite at the Wigwam Motel back in Iowa.

Andrew sat shivering on a bench; Jane pulled off his shoes and socks while Andrew struggled with the buttons on his shirt. His fingers were too cold and numb to undo the buttons so Jane unbuttoned and remove his shirt. Andrew unbuckled his belt and stood to remove his pants, but his pants were wet and clung to his legs. Jane pushed him back down on the bench, grabbed the ends of his pant legs and dragged the pants off. Andrew stood up, turned around, and managed to pull off his shorts, and make his way into the hot tub.

Jane went back to the jeep, retrieved their back packs, and also got a first aid kit from under the front seat. She went back to the cabin, stripped off her clothes, added them to Andrew's pile near the door, and joined Andrew in the hot tub.

The hot tub had already started the job of warming Andrew. He had stopped shivering, and his lips were back to their normal color.

"It seems just like old times at the Wigwam." Andrew said after soaking for a few minutes.

Jane replied, "I can't believe this. It's just too crazy. We even have a new 'Aunt Martha' who has us married again."

"Maybe the honeymoon suite cupids are trying to tell us something."

"I hope the little girl and her mother are OK." Jane said, changing the subject.

"I don't think they had any injuries, and I'm sure the EMT squad will take care of them."

"You are amazing. Everyone else was just standing around waiting for that car to get washed down the river, but you just grabbed the winch cable and jumped right in. I was afraid you were going to end up being washed away."

Jane reached over and stroked Andrew's cheek.

"I was really afraid I was going to lose you."

"I didn't have time to think about it. I just saw that woman waving from her car, and I thought I had to do something. I think if she and her daughter had been washed down the river, I would have had nightmares for a long time. If I think about what might have happened to them, or to me, I might have nightmares anyway."

There was a knock on the door and, without waiting for an answer, Martha came in with a tray loaded with chicken noodle soup, a thermos of hot tea, and two big slices of carrot cake.

"Now don't you pay me any attention. It looks like you've warmed up some. I was worried that you might get hypothermia if we didn't do something fast. Fortunately, the honeymoon cabin wasn't occupied.

"I'm just going to get these clothes to the laundry."

She picked up the clothes, emptied the pockets, put the contents on the desk, and looked over at Andrew.

"Young man, you just saved two lives, prevented a world of grief for the family, and risked your own life in the process. I don't see that kind of thing very often these days. You consider yourselves guests of the Drowsy Creek Lodge for as long as you like, and as often as you like."

Andrew said, "Thank you Aunt Martha." Jane tried to hide her giggle.

"You can call me Aunt Martha if you like; I don't mind a bit. I've been called worse in my day."

"I'm sorry." Andrew said, "That just sort of slipped out. It's kind of our inside joke. We had another motel experience recently where there was a nice lady who was also named Martha. She reminded me of my Aunt Annie's next door neighbor, who is named Martha, and we started referring to her as 'Aunt Martha.' It seems that we have been blessed with several 'Aunt Marthas' in our lives."

"I guess I'll take that as a compliment. I'm going to get these clothes washed and dried. You'll find them in a laundry bag by the front door in the morning. If you need anything else, just dial 0 on the phone. I'm going to lock the door now and won't be bothering you any more tonight."

Andrew and Jane soaked in the hot tub for awhile. Finally, Jane said, "I'm going to take a shower. I feel like I have sand in my hair."

"That's a good idea. I think I'll join you."

Jane didn't bother to object, and they got into the shower and washed each other's backs.

"You have a nasty rope burn around your waist from the winch cable."

Jane lightly felt the bruise around Andrew's waist.

"I don't see any broken skin. You still have a couple of spots from the cactus thorns. After we have our soup, I'm going to apply some first aid cream to those spots."

They dried off and put on the bathrobes.

"These are nice, but they aren't pink and blue like the ones at the Wigwam."

They sat at the small table where Martha had put the tray with the soup. They discovered they were very hungry and polished it off in short order; then they attacked the carrot cake.

Sighing, Jane said, "I think I could get used to this kind of living. Now let me see to those old cactus wounds."

Andrew took off the bathrobe and laid face down on the bed while Jane gently rubbed first aid cream over the spots made by the cactus.

"Ummm... Now this is something I could get used to."

Andrew rolled over and reached out, and pulled on Jane's bathrobe belt."

"Do you think we're ready for this?" She said,

"I've been ready for this ever since I met you on the train."

Jane slid the robe off her shoulders and joined Andrew on the bed.

The next morning, they took another slow shower together. Jane carefully opened the outside door and found a laundry bag containing their nicely folded clothes. They got dressed, straightened up the room, and then went to the office to properly thank Martha.

Martha gave them a knowing smile, "I'm just glad I could do something helpful. I hope you found the cabin was acceptable. Remember, you have an open invitation to stay at Drowsy Creek Lodge whenever you like."

"Thanks again... 'Aunt Martha'." Andrew said,

---

Getting into the jeep, they headed back toward Elk Park Ranch.

As they drove, Jane said, "I was so interested in your telling me about the interview with Amos Shipler, that I forgot to tell you about my interview with Ranger Bob."

"When was that?"

"It was the day of your interview with Amos Shipler. Bob called and asked me to meet him at the Kawuneeche Visitor Center. He said that one of the staff members had decided to retire, and that would free up the budget to hire someone. He asked if I would like to join the staff as a naturalist."

"What about your plan to go back to college?"

"I have to do some serious thinking. The reason for taking more courses is because I was hoping it would help me get on with the National Park Service. But the Kawuneeche job would get me in the door. I'd be doing staff work at the Visitor's Center, would be leading nature hikes, and would be in a place where I could apply for research grants through the NPS system."

"So what did you tell Bob?"

"He wasn't actually offering me a job. He was just feeling me out to see if I was interested. If he had a strong candidate for a position, it would influence how the job description would be posted. He just asked me to give it some thought and let him know my thinking in the next couple of weeks."

"And have you decided what to do?"

"I'm thinking, I'm thinking... Right now I'm just not ready to go back to the ranch. Let's stop in at the Granby Medical Center and find out how the mother and daughter are doing. Then what do you say we drive over to Fraser? There's a place there that has great barbecue."

"Sounds like a good plan to me."

When they arrived at the Granby Medical Center, they asked at the desk if they knew anything about the mother and daughter rescued from the flood. They were directed to the social services case manager. Finding the office, Jane approached the lady identified by her name tag as social services councilor.

"We're wondering if you have any information about the mother and daughter who were rescued from the flash flood yesterday."

"Are you relatives?"

"No, but Andrew was the one who pulled them out of the water. We simply want to know if they're all right."

"The EMT crew told us how they were rescued. You were clever and very brave to wade out to them with that winch cable. We understand that if you'd been a couple of minutes later, they would've been swept down the river.

"They suffered from mild hypothermia and were treated and kept here overnight for observation. The husband was here this morning and checked them out; you just missed them. I think they're trying to arrange transportation, so they might still be in the lounge.

"They wanted to know about the man who rescued them so that they could thank him. Mary, the little girl, asked who the nice man was who carried her out of the water.

"Ordinarily I'm not supposed to release any information about patients, but this is a special case. And, I might add, not a very happy one. Their names are Maria and Mary Sandoval; the husband is Luis Sandoval. They're living in a trailer up near Winter Park.

"They don't have medical insurance. Luis has a seasonal job at the Winter Park ski area and isn't covered by health insurance. They have a large unpaid medical bill because of Mary's tonsillectomy last winter. Now, on top of everything else, they've lost their car, and there's a large balance on their car loan. They bought it at one of those 'buy here pay here' car lots that seem to prey on poor people.

"I've been working with some of the social service agencies here in Grand County to see if we can find them some help. Maria works as a part time housekeeper at a ski lodge, but they lay off most of their workers in the off season. Luis finds temporary jobs here and there in the off season. Anyway, that's their story. Thank you, Andrew, for rescuing them, and I really appreciate the fact that you came by to see how they're doing. I'm sorry I troubled you with their problems. Sometimes I get too involved with some of the cases I have to deal with."

"Thank you for sharing. I'm sure that you have made a positive difference in a lot of lives. Keep up the good work."

As they walked down the hall from the social services office, Jane suggested they check the lounge to see if Maria and Mary were still there. As they entered the lounge, little Mary spotted them and shouted, "There's the man who pulled me out of the water."

She ran over, jumped up on Andrew, and gave him a big hug.

"Mary, it's not polite to jump on people like that."

"But he came and pulled us out of the water so we didn't die. You told that lady you wanted to thank him."

"Yes, but you can thank him without attacking him. I'm sorry about that, sir. My name is Maria and I guess now you know Mary. I'm glad you're here so I can properly thank you for saving us."

"My name is Andrew, and this is Jane. We're very glad that you're both OK after the scary business with the flood."

Luis came over, introduced himself, and shook Andrew's hand.

"I'm Luis, Mary's father and Maria's husband. I can't tell you how grateful I am to you. I wish there was some way I could pay you for what you've done for my family."

"Luis, seeing that Mary and Maria were not seriously injured, and seeing you together as a family is all the thanks I need."

Jane interrupted, "The social services lady said you are arranging transportation."

"Well, as you know, our car is gone. I managed to hitchhike here when I got a call about Maria and Mary. One of the security guards lives up in Fraser, and he said he could give us a ride home when his shift is over."

"When is his shift over?"

"He gets off at six this afternoon."

"Andrew and I were on our way to Fraser to get something to eat. Maybe we could give you a ride."

"That would be very nice of you, but we already owe you too much."

"Nonsense. We're going that way anyway. It's no problem for us to give you a ride."

"That would be nice. Let me tell the security guard we found a ride."

As they all headed for the Jeep, Mary was still hugging Andrew around his neck, the same way she had when he was carrying her out of the river.

"It looks like you have a new girlfriend Andrew. Should I be jealous?"

"Maybe you should be. She might just be a little cuter than you, but she's too short for me."

As they approached the outskirts of Fraser, Jane said she was hungry and suggested stopping for lunch. Andrew agreed. Luis and Maria said they were not that far from their trailer and could walk the rest of the way home.

Jane asked, "Did you have anything to eat at the hospital today?"

"No." Maria admitted.

"Let's just stop at Carl's Diner and you can join us for lunch."

"Don't worry about the bill, lunch is on me." Andrew said.

"You don't need to do this." Luis protested.

"Yes I do. When the magazine I was working for closed down, the owner gave all of the employees a big severance payment, all the staff moved on and I never had a chance to celebrate my windfall. So now that I have Mary as my new girlfriend, let me make this my celebration."

They found a table at Carl's Diner. Jane and Maria ordered the chef's salad, Mary said she would like a Carl's Junior Bacon Cheeseburger with tater tots, and

Andrew and Luis ordered a Carl's Deluxe Burger with french fries.

Jane asked them about their jobs.

Luis replied, "Right now, I'm looking for something.

"In the winter it's easy to find work, but in the off season it's hard to find anything. I usually can find a temporary job to keep us going. I'm willing to take on most anything, even though sometimes I don't like the kind of jobs I have to take."

Maria added, "I'm in the same boat. The reason I ended up in the flash flood was I had been over to Hot Sulphur Springs to put in some applications. I don't very often drive that far from home. It was on the way back that the car was caught in the flash flood."

Maria choked back a sob as she recalled the car being carried into the river.

Jane tore off a piece of the place mat and asked Maria to write down her phone number and address.

"I work at Elk Park Ranch, and sometimes we hear of openings. They also sometimes post job openings on the bulletin board at the general store where I shop. If I see anything, I'll let you know."

She tore off another piece and wrote her name and phone number and handed it to Maria.

"Please give me call if I can help you with anything. Sometimes after a terrifying experience like the one you had with the flood, it's good to talk about it with someone. I know what it's like. I was attacked recently, and I still get the shakes thinking about it. I don't know what I would have done if I didn't have friends to talk to."

When he heard Jane mention the recent attack, Luis sucked in his breath and recalled the girl Butch had attacked when they'd poached the sheep.

Andrew got out his wallet to pay the bill and shrugged off Luis protests.

"Remember, I told you this one is on me."

The group got back in the jeep and followed Maria's directions to their trailer home located a little ways away. Andrew noticed an older model pickup truck parked beside the trailer.

"Is that your truck?"

Luis nodded, "Yes, that's mine. The oil pan cracked, the oil drained out, and the engine seized up. We haven't been able to save enough money yet to get it repaired."

"That's tough." Andrew replied.

After dropping the Sandoval family at their trailer, Jane put the jeep in gear and headed back toward

Grand Lake and the ranch. She frowned, "Doesn't your heart just go out for that family?"

"I know. It makes me want to try to do something to help them, but Luis is a proud man and I don't think he's comfortable taking charity from people. I hope the social services lady at the medical center can arrange for some help for them."

"Maybe there might be some jobs at the ranch. If I decide to accept Bob's offer to go to work for the NPS, the ranch would need to replace me."

"I hope your do-gooder urge doesn't override your need to find your own career goals."

"You're right, of course. I still have some serious thinking to do about what I want to do next, and that NPS job sounds attractive."

## Chapter 20 - Butch Investigates

After he received the call from Dr. Tex Frey, Butch sat for awhile in Dante's Bar and slowly added to a growing line of empty Coors bottles. He was in a quandary; he understood why Tex was worried about witnesses. If his poaching ring was exposed, or stopped, Tex stood to lose a lot of money.

The question bothering Butch was "if he was able to identify any possible witnesses, what then?" He was a big game hunter, not a hired killer. He had no qualms about violating hunting regulations in pursuit of a trophy. His enjoyment in life, besides having money in his pocket to spend, was the thrill of the hunt. He had never thought of himself as an assassin or hired murderer.

Butch recalled Tex's comments about the sunbather before they'd discovered she had disappeared. Tex had said something like, "Maybe she might just have a riding accident." At the time, the comment made Butch uncomfortable, and he had felt a little relieved that the girl had gotten away. Knowing that Tex now wanted him to find her, and find another possible witness, was troublesome.

Maybe he was worrying too much; Tex had a lot of money. Maybe he was just planning to pay off witnesses, or maybe threaten them into silence. Tex might even try to threaten him into silence if he refused to follow orders. Did Tex have anything that he could use to pressure him to do his nasty work for him? Unlike Luis, who had a family to protect, there was no one in Butch's life that could be used to force Butch to do anything.

What else could Text hold over him? He knew Tex could probably produce a lot of evidence that would point to Butch's poaching activities. The more he thought about it, he recalled the times when Tex had insisted that Butch pose with the kills for pictures. Was Tex doing that as insurance to force Butch's silence? Butch knew stories about severe punishment handed out to poachers. Fines had been levied that went well into five figures. Guns and hunting equipment, and even vehicles had been confiscated. There were also stories of poachers being given jail sentences.

Butch decided he'd better make an effort to find out what had happened to the sunbather. He'd have to make a trip to the Grand Lake area and ask around. But how could he do that without raising suspicions? Then he remembered that Luis lived near Winter Park, not too far from Grand Lake.

The next day, Butch made a call to Luis. Maria answered the phone.

"Hello."

"Is Luis home? I need to speak to him."

"Can I say who is calling?"

"Just tell him I have some work for him."

Maria found Luis working on his pickup truck. He knew he wouldn't be able to fix it himself, but he hoped that if he could do some of the disassembly, he might be able to get a lower price for the repair.

"Luis, you have a phone call."

"Who is it? I have my hands full of grease right now."

"He didn't give his name. He said he had some work for you."

Luis wiped his hands on a dirty rag, and picked up the phone, "Hello, who is this?"

"This is your hunting friend. I have a job for you. You need to call me back from a phone where your wife can't hear you. Call me at this number at 7:30."

Butch read off the phone number and Luis wrote it down.

"I can't do that right now. I don't have transportation."

"It's in your interest to call me. You know what might happen to your family if you don't cooperate."

"I'll try, but you must know it's difficult for me right now."

"Just make the call at 7:30."

Butch broke the connection and Luis hung up.

"Who was that, Luis?"

"Just some guy I worked with a while back."

"Does he have a job for you? We really need the money."

"I know how much we need money!" Luis snapped, "Just let me take care of this. I'm going to have to go out for a while this evening."

Maria frowned. Luis didn't usually speak to her that way. She wondered if he was in some kind of trouble.

After dinner, Luis said, "I'm going out." He ignored Maria's question about where he was going. It was several blocks through the trailer park to Route 40.

Once he got to Route 40, he walked a little over a mile to a Phillips 66 gas station where there was a pay phone. He bought a candy bar, got some change for the phone, and made the call to Butch.

"This is Luis. I'm calling from a pay phone so if this call is going to take very long, you'll have to call me back at this number."

Butch was annoyed. Who did Luis think he was, anyway. He went ahead and returned the call to the number Luis had given him.

Luis grabbed the phone as soon as it rang.

"This is Luis."

"You've got some nerve treating me like you're somebody important."

"What do you expect? You didn't want me to talk in front of Maria, and I don't have one of those mansions with lots of phones everywhere."

"OK, OK! Listen, the boss has a job that needs your help. You remember the sunbather from the last sheep hunt?"

"Yes, what about her?"

"The boss thinks someone must have untied her and that means there is probably more than one witness. He wants you to find out what happened to the girl, and find out who let her loose."

"Why me?"

"Because you live close to Grand Lake, and you can go there and ask around."

"I can't do that."

"Why not?"

"Because I don't have any transportation. My wife got caught in a flash flood and our car got washed down the river."

"That's your problem, not mine. Hitchhike, or steal a car if you have to. You need to get up there, find out what happened to that girl, and report back to me. If you don't, you should remember that you have a pretty wife and a cute little girl. I'd hate to see something bad happen to them. Get me some answers soon."

Butch slammed down the phone. He cursed Luis under his breath, and then went back to lining up Coors bottles at Dante's.

Luis bought himself a couple of sticks of Jack Links beef jerky, a coke, and sat down on a bench in front of the Phillips 66 station to think things over.

Luis thought back to the lunch with Andrew and Jane. He remembered Jane's comment about having been recently attacked. Jane worked at Elk Park Ranch, and that was just down the valley from the sheep kill. It was possible Jane was the sunbather.

He also remembered Tex saying the girl Butch had tied up maybe could have a horseback riding accident. He hadn't liked it when Tex said that. It was clear Tex was willing to hurt the girl. What if that girl was Jane? Andrew and Jane were obviously pretty close. What if Andrew was the one who had untied her?

Luis was torn. Even if the witnesses Tex was trying to find were not Jane and Andrew, whoever they were would be in danger if Tex found them. If something bad happened to them, he would be at least partly responsible.

On the other hand, if he did not report back to Butch with the names of the witnesses, he would be putting Maria and Mary in danger. Luis put his hands on the back of his head, pulling his head down over his knees in frustration. A customer coming out of the Phillips 66 station stopped and asked if he was OK.

"I'm all right."

But he knew he was far from all right. He finally decided he had to tell Maria what was going on and slowly walked back to the trailer.

---

"Where have you been? What's wrong with you? You have to tell me."

"I hope you're not going to hate me, but I'm in a bad situation and I don't know what to do."

"You know I love you. Please tell me what's going on."

Luis told Maria the whole story, from the sheep poaching to the phone call from Butch.

"If it was Jane that was attacked by Butch, and if Tex finds out it was her, he might do something bad. Even if I find out it was some other girl and tell Butch, some other girl will get hurt, or maybe even killed, and I'll be responsible. If I don't call Butch back with some information, then you and Mary will be in danger. There's a lot of money involved in this poaching business, and these guys are ruthless. I just don't know what to do."

Maria gave Luis a hug, and tried to hide her tears. They sat like this for quite a while. Finally Maria said, "Why don't I talk to Jane. Maybe she can help."

"I don't see how she can possibly help. If we tell her I was involved in poaching, she might report me, and then I'd probably end up in jail."

"At least we should warn her. Do you have any better idea?"

"No."

"I can't think of how I would live if you were in jail, but I think Jane reporting you for poaching is a chance we have to take. Tomorrow I'm going to call her."

The next morning Maria made the call.

"Hello Jane, this is Maria."

"Hi Maria."

"I want to thank you and Andrew again for your help."

"That's OK, we were glad to help."

"Do you remember you said if I needed to talk to someone, I could call you?"

"Yes, and I meant it. I'm ready to listen to whatever you need to talk about."

"Luis and I need to talk to someone about a very serious problem we have, and it's possible it might involve you and it might also involve Andrew."

"OK, you have my attention. What's this all about?"

"I don't think we can do this over the phone. It's too complicated, and both Luis and I have to talk to you together. I'd like to meet somewhere, but as you know, we don't have transportation."

"Why don't Andrew and I take a ride to your place? Would this afternoon be OK?"

"That would be very good. I can't tell you how much I appreciate everything you've done for us."

"Can we meet around noon at Carl's Diner?"

"Yes, it's close, we can walk there from here."

"We'll see you soon."

Jane found Andrew talking with Ned, who was giving him a lecture on the care and feeding of horses.

"Hi Ned. I see you've found a new victim for one of your famous monologues."

"Always appreciate having a good listener around to chew the jerky with."

"Ned has been trying to sign me up as a new horse wrangler. He claims managing the livestock and maintaining the grounds is getting to be too big a job for an old guy like him, and he needs some help."

"I never yet met a man who didn't claim he was overworked and under paid. It must be in men's genes. I'm afraid I'm going to steal, or maybe rescue, Andrew. I have something we need to talk about."

"Sounds serious to me. Let me know if you want to sign on as a wrangler, Andrew."

Jane led Andrew to her cabin.

"Did you bring me here to seduce me again?"

"Sorry Andrew, we don't have time for that right now. Something has come up with Maria and Luis."

"What is it?"

"I'm not sure. Maria called me and sounded very upset. She said she and Luis had to talk to us and it's too complicated to talk about over the phone; she wants us to meet. I agreed we would meet them at Carl's Diner this afternoon. I hope that's OK with you."

"Of course it is. Do you have any idea what this is all about?"

"She said they had a serious problem that might involve us."

"Do you think it could have something to do with the flash flood incident?"

"I just don't know. We'll just have to wait until we see them to find out. It's a little less than an hour's drive from here. I have to let Marge know I won't be working this afternoon. Meet me at the office at around 11."

On the jeep ride to Carl's Diner, there wasn't much they could say about the mysterious meeting Maria had requested. As they drove along the shores of Shadow Mountain Reservoir and Lake Granby, Jane told Andrew a little about how water from the west slope was trapped in the lakes and then sent across the continental divide to irrigate farms to the east of the mountains. The water falling down the east slope to a lower elevation was cleverly used to generate power to pump the water out of the lakes.

Jane pointed to a collection of docks and boats, and told Andrew they were looking at the highest elevation yacht club in the world.

When they got to Carl's Diner, they found Luis and Maria waiting for them.

"Where's Mary?" Andrew asked.

"One of the waitresses is a friend of mine." Maria replied, "She's giving Mary some drawing lessons in the break room."

Jane asked, "So what's up?

Maria took the lead, "Before we start, Jane, we need to know if you were the one who was attacked and had her horse stolen?"

"Yes, I was."

"Was Andrew the one who rescued you?"

"Yes, he was. But what does that have to do with your problem?"

"Luis thinks both of you are in danger. We're afraid when Luis tells you why he thinks that, you might have to report him, and he'll be arrested. But we don't have a choice; we don't know where else to turn. Luis, tell them what you told me about the trouble we're in."

Luis told the story; starting with needing a job, and that even though he knew poaching was wrong, he went along with it because he needed the money. He said he'd been with the poachers when Jane was attacked.

Jane interrupted, "Are you saying you know who the poachers are, and that you can identify them?"

"Yes."

Luis continued to tell them what he had told Maria earlier. He finished by once again describing how he was feeling trapped with no way out. He had to either choose to do something that might cause harm to Jane and Andrew, or do nothing and put Maria and Mary in danger.

Jane said, "I have to make a phone call. Don't worry, Luis. I'm not calling the police, and I'm not reporting you. I know someone who might be able to keep you out of jail."

Andrew said he would see if there was a phone Jane could use. He found the waitress and asked if he could talk to the manager. She disappeared in the back of the diner and returned with a man wearing an apron.

"I'm Carl, the owner. Do you want to complain about the food?"

"No, everything is fine. I want to know if you have a phone my friend can use for a private call."

He got out his wallet and took out a twenty dollar bill.

"I'll be happy to pay whatever you want for the use of your phone for a long distance call. I know this is an unusual request, but we have a situation where a number of people may be in danger."

"Put your money away. I don't charge for helping people out. The phone's in the office."

Andrew motioned for Jane to come over, and Carl showed her into the office and closed the office door.

"I really appreciate this. While we're waiting for Jane to make her call, we should order lunch."

Carl asked the waitress to take their order and went back to the kitchen. Andrew returned to the table.

"We might as well have lunch while we're waiting for Jane."

Luis was sitting with his elbows on the table and his head in his hands.

"I'm sorry for causing so much trouble. I was just trying to make some money to pay our bills. Instead, I end up hurting people."

"No one's been hurt yet. Jane's uncle is the one who is heading up the poaching investigation. It was his suggestion we report the attack on Jane as horse stealing instead of poaching, to keep the poachers from being tipped off that the authorities were after them. Come on, Luis, you have to eat something."

They ordered the same things as on their previous visit to Carl's. Meanwhile, Jane was on the phone to her Uncle Bill.

"Jane, how are things going over there?"

"Uncle Bill, I have someone who can identify the poachers. However, I need to know if you can offer him immunity from prosecution."

"Wait a minute. Are you saying you know one of the poachers?"

"Well, yes and no. I know who he is, and he was with the poachers when the sheep were killed, but he is not really a poacher. He got tangled up with them because he desperately needs money for his family. He's a good man who's in trouble and wants to do the right thing, even if it means going to jail.

"The poachers apparently decided someone must have rescued me, and believe there may be two witnesses. They want my contact to find out what happened to the sunbather and identify her (that means me) and her rescuer. They've threatened to harm his wife and daughter if he doesn't report back to them soon. My contact is convinced that by confessing to his part in the sheep killing, he'll end up in jail. What I want to know is, can you promise him immunity if he identifies the poachers?"

"If this guy can actually identify the poachers, I'll do my best to keep him out of jail. From what you just told me, the poachers are out for blood. You and Andrew are in real danger now. Apparently your contact and his family might also be in danger. But we'll need a solid case against these poachers before we can move on them."

"I'm thinking that the poachers don't yet know about Andrew and me, and our association with Elk Park Ranch. Why don't I contact Marge at the ranch and see if she'd let my contact and his family stay there? That way he would be available to your task force for an interview, and his family would be protected?"

"Sounds like a plan. In the meantime, I'll see what I can do about this immunity thing. By the way, good work."

"There is no good work about this at all. It's all just a complicated collection of coincidences. Some day, I'll tell you the whole story."

As soon as she said good bye to Bill, Jane called Marge at the ranch.

"Marge, this is Jane."

"Jane, where are you?"

"I'm with Andrew. We're with a family that needs our help. I'll explain it all later. Is that old wrangler cabin over by the horse barn still empty?"

"Yes, but it hasn't been used for a while, and it's kind of dirty."

"Would it be OK if we allowed a young couple and their daughter to stay there for a while. Their names are Maria and Luis. Their daughter Mary is 5 or 6 years old. I'm sure Maria could help with housekeeping and Luis could help Ned with the horses or grounds keeping. We wouldn't have to put them on the payroll."

"Come on Jane, what's this all about?"

"I can't explain over the phone. Just that they're in danger, and they don't have any money to go anywhere else."

"OK, I'll trust you on this."

"Thanks, Marge. You don't know how much help you're providing. I promise to tell you the whole story some day. For now, let's say they are new staff members."

Jane stopped in the kitchen to thank Carl and tell him she was through using the phone. On the way back to the table to join the group, she went past the staff break room and saw Mary busily drawing.

"Hi Mary. It looks like you're a real artist."

"Hi Jane. I'm making a drawing of the flood."

Jane rejoined the group.

"Luis, I talked to my Uncle Bill. He has an important job with the poacher investigation team and will try to get immunity for you if you can identify the poachers and possibly testify against them. I know you're very worried about the safety of your family. I talked to Marge, the owner of Elk Park Ranch. There's an old cabin on the ranch where your family can stay until this is over.

"You'll be interviewed by someone from the team investigating the poachers. In the meantime, I'm hoping you'll help Ned, who manages the stables and does grounds-keeping. Maria, if you're willing, you can help the housekeeping staff with cleaning.

"What do you say? Are you ready to hide out at the ranch until this blows over? It will mean you'll have to leave your trailer for now. If Luis is right, the poachers might come looking for you there."

Luis was speechless. Maria looked at Jane with tears in her eyes.

"We can never repay you for all of this. It's more than we could ever expect."

"None of us will be completely safe until the poachers are locked away. But at least we have a plan to get all of us through the next few days."

Mary came out from the break room holding a picture.

"This my drawing of the big flood. See, there is Andrew carrying me to the jeep, and Mommy is holding his belt like a trailer. And that's our car floating like a boat going down the river."

Andrew took the picture and made a big display of studying it.

"I didn't know you were such a good artist, Mary. I think we should frame it and hang it in a special place."

Maria pulled Mary onto her lap.

"Mary, we've decided to leave our trailer for a while. We're going to stay at a ranch."

"Do they have horses and everything?"

Jane replied, "Yes, they have horses and everything, even a swimming pool. But this is a working ranch. You might even have to help with the chores."

"That's OK. Daddy always says we have to work for what we get."

Andrew paid the check, and they all went out to the jeep.

As soon as Bill hung up after Jane's call, he went into action. He set up a conference call with everyone from the investigation team.

"It looks like we just got a big break. My niece Jane has made contact with a member of the poacher gang. If we can grant him immunity from prosecution, we can get him to identify the poachers and testify in court if it comes to that. He says that his family has been threatened if he doesn't continue to cooperate with the poaches. Jane found a safe house for the family. Let's go around the group, and see where we are in the investigation."

Different members of the task force reported.

"The saddle was analyzed, and we found fingerprints from two unidentified individuals."

"We have a group of hikers who noticed an unusual pickup truck at the trail head the day of the poaching. They noticed it because most hikers don't drive large crew cab pickups. We really got lucky; the hikers had taken pictures of themselves in the parking lot, and one of the pictures shows a black Ford crew cab pickup truck. Unfortunately, the license plate wasn't visible in the picture."

"Our Game Warden in Alamosa reports that one of his Manassa contacts saw a large black SUV stopped outside of Rob Role's taxidermy shop the day after the poaching incident. Manassa is a small town and the locals know all of the local vehicles, so any strange vehicles get their attention. The contact was a dog walker who saw the SUV when she walked past the shop, but it was gone by the time she went around the block and returned."

"Our ballistics experts have analyzed the bullet taken from one of the sheep, and the cartridge found near the site. They've determined the weapon used was a Blaser R93. The marks on the bullet will allow for a positive match if we can locate the weapon."

Bill took over the conversation.

"If we can get these guys, it looks like we have enough evidence to put them away. We know the poachers are actively trying to identify witnesses to the sheep kill. We have to assume our witnesses and our informant and his family are in danger from these poachers. We have to get them before they hurt, or even kill people.

"We need to get an interview with Jane's contact as soon as possible, and we need to be prepared to provide him immunity from prosecution for his testimony. His family has apparently been threatened by the poachers. We need to find a way to protect them without tipping off the poachers as to their whereabouts.

"Grand Lake is a small town, and although a lot of tourists come through there, the locals know what is going on and who belongs there and who doesn't. I'll contact Amos Shipler, the local newspaper owner, and see if he can quietly initiate a kind of neighborhood watch for our suspects.

"We need to get a search of automobile registrations for the west slope and see if we can find a Ford pickup truck matching the one in the hiker snapshot.

"If one of the poachers is from out-of-state, there's a chance the black SUV seen in Manassa was rented from the Denver airport. We need to check the rental records for the days before and after the sheep kill, and check the mileage of returned SUV s. We can calculate the mileage from the airport to Grand Lake, down to Manassa and back to Denver, and try to match it with rental records.

"I'd like the State Patrol special investigations unit to send a couple of unmarked cars to Grand Lake and be on the lookout for both the Ford pickup and a black SUV. We need to be in radio contact with them so we can move fast if we get a lead on the poachers. OK, let's get these guys."

"Hello, Shipler here."

"Hello Amos, Bill Rutherfield. I'm calling to give you an update on our poacher investigation. By the way, thanks for keeping the poaching incident out of the news."

"I appreciate being informed about anything going on in my neighborhood. You know we always work together on this sort of thing."

Bill provided Amos with a status report on the investigation. He asked Amos to keep his eyes and ears open for anything happening in Grand Lake.

"We know that the poachers are trying to identify witnesses to the sheep killing and horse stealing. It looks like Jane and Andrew might be in real danger. We need to stop these guys before they can hurt anyone. By the way, do you know anything about the Sandoval family?"

"Yes, of course. I believe that the mother and daughter were the ones caught in the flash flood."

"That's correct. We have information that the poachers may also try to hurt the mother and daughter.

It turns out Luis Sandoval has gotten crossways with the poachers, and they've threatened his family. The family is hiding out at Elk Park Ranch.

"We suspect that one of the poachers is driving a black Ford crew cab pickup. Another might be driving a black SUV. The SUV might have a rental car sticker on it. Keep all of this under your hat for now. I know you have eyes everywhere in your turf. Let me know if you discover anything."

Amos called Jerry Peterson at the general store and asked him to be on the lookout for anyone asking about the horse stealing, and not to tell anyone whose horse was stolen. He passed the same message on to several other dependable business owners in town.

## Chapter 21 - The Sandovals Move In

Jane and Andrew took the Sandoval family to their trailer. While they were packing the personal items necessary for an extended visit to the ranch, Jane suggested that Maria call the phone company and cancel their service. She hoped this might make it harder for the poachers to find them. If they called, and got a 'not in service' message, it might convince them the Sandoval's had left the area.

They loaded everything into the jeep and drove back to the ranch. In the office, they were greeted by Marge.

"Marge, this is the family I was telling you about. This is Luis, and his wife Maria, and daughter Mary."

"Welcome to Elk Park Ranch. I'm pleased to meet you all."

Luis and Maria shook hands. Luis said, "We can't thank you enough for letting us stay here. I hate to be a beggar, but we really didn't know where to turn until Jane suggested that we might be able to stay here for awhile."

"You don't have to be a beggar here. If you're willing, there's always plenty of work to do around the ranch, and we can always use extra help."

"Thank you. We'll do anything you ask us to do."

"The first thing to do is go to your cabin; Ned and Nancy are there trying to get it ready for you. It hasn't been used for a while, so it's not in the best condition."

Maria offered, "Please let us help. I'm a good housekeeper, and Luis is very handy at fixing things. We don't want charity. We're happy to work to pay our way."

Andrew moved the jeep to the cabin where it was easier to unload, while Marge led a small parade to the cabin. They were introduced to Nancy and Ned.

Nancy apologized, "I'm sorry this place is such a mess. I'm afraid the spiders and mice have taken over."

Ned chimed in, "You can't see the spiders through the windows. They haven't been washed in years. It's embarrassing for us to have our guests see it like this, but we didn't have much warning about your coming."

"Ned, I'm sorry to pull a surprise on you like this, but the Sandoval's aren't regular ranch guests. They're going to be helping out around here for a while." Marge responded.

Luis volunteered, "If you show us the tools and cleaning supplies, we'll help with the cleaning. I'll start with the windows and Maria will take care of the inside. We don't want to interfere with your regular work."

The four of them, Ned, Nancy, Maria, and Luis dug into the project, with Mary chasing spiders and looking for mice. The cabin was soon ready for them to move in.

Jane motioned to Marge to follow her back to the office to talk; Andrew unloaded the jeep and joined them.

Jane told Marge as much about the Sandoval's situation as she could without getting into anything about the poachers.

"Remember when Andrew rescued the mother and daughter from the flood? Well, that was Maria and Mary. Andrew and I went to the Granby Medical Center to see how they were doing. We met with the social services coordinator and she told us a little about the Sandoval family. Luis and Maria work at seasonal jobs and have little or no income during the off season. They don't have health insurance, and have a large outstanding debt from Mary's tonsillectomy last year.

"Their car, not paid for, was lost in the flash flood. Luis has an old pickup truck that blew it's engine, and they don't have money to repair it. We met them in the lounge area of the Medical Center where they were trying to find a ride back to their trailer. It's parked between Fraser and Winter Park.

"We gave them a ride, stopped for lunch with them along the way, and learned a little more about their background. They are not deadbeats or welfare parasites; they're trying hard to make it on their own. Luis is a very proud man, and it's very difficult for him to accept charity. We learned that someone who Luis once worked with is trying to force him to do something questionable, and Luis is refusing. This guy threatened Louis by suggesting bad things would happen to Maria and Mary if Luis refuses his request.

"We think they're in real danger, and that's why we asked you to let them stay here until the problem is resolved. However, we have to be on the lookout for any strangers in the area. Hopefully, the bad guys won't be able to trace the Sandoval family to here. I'm expecting a law enforcement officer to come by to interview Luis. Otherwise, we have to be on our guard."

"I can see how you got involved in this, Jane. I know how softhearted you are. That little girl is darling, and anyone would want to protect her."

"You should have seen how she greeted Andrew at the Medical Center. She jumped right up into his arms and gave him a big thank you hug for pulling her out of the water."

Marge smiled, "It seems Andrew is always ready to jump in and help when needed. I think you did the right thing in bringing the Sandovals here. The Sandovals certainly need help, and they seem to be willing to work. I'll talk to the staff about them, without revealing too many details. I think we can help them out."

Marge gave them a grin, "It looks like you and Andrew have become quite a team. It's nice to see that. I've been trying to get Jane to join a team for quite a while."

—————————————————

Two plain gray cars from the State Patrol special investigations unit arrived in Grand Lake; one of them parked in the lot near the Conoco station on Route 34. The only way in and out of Grand Lake is Route 34 which comes from Granby, continues through Rocky Mountain National Park, over Trail Ridge Road, and on to the east. If the poachers were driving, it's unlikely they would be using Trail Ridge Road. The Conoco station parking lot provided a view of all cars coming into Grand Lake from Granby.

The other special investigations car went on to Elk Park Ranch to interview Luis.

One of the plain clothes officers went into the office, identified himself to Marge, and asked to see Luis Sandoval.

"We've been expecting you. He's probably in his cabin. Let me show you the way."

Luis was actually not in his cabin, but was within sight. He was helping Ned repair some fence posts on the corral.

"Luis, This man is here to interview you. Maybe he could do it in your cabin."

Ned was curious, but didn't say anything. Maria and Mary were working on a flower bed in front of the cabin. Mary greeted Marge.

"Hi Marge, look what me and Mom are doing. Mom's cleaning up the flower bed and I'm the official weed puller."

"Hi Mary, good job! That's looking very nice, Maria. This gentleman is here to interview Luis. They'll be using the cabin for a while."

Luis held the door open for the investigator, and offered him a seat at the kitchen table. The investigator showed Luis his credentials.

"Do you know why I'm here?" he asked.

"I expect you want to know about the big horn sheep poaching."

"That's correct. Before we start, I want you to know that you are not being charged with anything. You should not make any formal confession about anything, or mention anything about your personal involvement in poaching activities. Our meeting here is simply to gather facts that will tell us who killed the sheep.

If you were being charged with a crime, I would have to read you your rights, and advise you that you could request the presence of a lawyer. Actually, since the sheep were killed in the National Park, it's technically out of my jurisdiction to arrest you anyway. I am only here to gather evidence for the poaching case. Do you understand?"

"Do you mean that you're not here to arrest me?"

"No, I'm not. So please relax. Just tell me as much as you can about what you know about the men who killed the sheep."

Luis breathed out a sigh of relief, "I was afraid you were going to take me to jail."

"We won't do that. As a matter of fact, we've put a team in place that have, as a part of their job, to protect you and your family."

The investigator took out a small tape recorder, and placed it on the table.

"Just so you know, I'm going to record this interview. Is that OK with you?"

Luis nodded and said yes. The investigator pushed the record button. "Now, please tell me as much as you can about the poachers."

"The man who threatened me and my family is named Butch. I'm afraid I don't know his last name; he does all of the dirty work. He scouts out the animals ahead of time to make it easier for the kill. He arranges for all of the local things like supplies or whatever. I think Butch lives somewhere around Frisco. Here's his phone number."

Luis pulled out a scrap of paper with the number and handed it to the investigator.

"When things are ready, he calls someone he calls the Boss. I'm afraid I don't know the name of the Boss; I don't think he lives around here. I think he might be from Texas; he sounds like a Texan, but not like someone who grew up in Texas. He arranged for us… I mean he arranged for Butch to pick him up from his car so they could ride together in Butch's pickup truck. I think his car had a rental sticker on it."

Luis paused for a moment and tried hard to concentrate. He needed to tell about Butch and the

Boss without making himself part of the story. He tried to imagine himself in an airplane looking down at things; he continued.

"Butch and the Boss parked at one of the trail head parking lots in the Park. They were wearing hiking clothes to look like hikers. When we...I mean when they got near where Butch had located the sheep, they left the trail. A little ways off the trail they changed into camo suits.

"Butch pulled a case out of his back pack. The Boss opened it and assembled a sniper rifle. He attached a silencer, and a scope. They then climbed up onto a ridge where they could see some big rams across a gulch, and higher up the mountain. The Boss picked off two of the rams that fell down into the gulch. The Boss is pretty good with that sniper rifle; because it was about a 300 yard shot.

"While the Boss was putting his rifle back in the case, Butch noticed someone on a horse riding up the trail. As they watched, the rider, a girl, went off the trail to a small clearing, tied the horse, rolled out a blanket, and started sunbathing.

"Butch was a little upset and figured they would have to abandon the kill, but the Boss thought they could take the horse and use it to pack out the sheep. He sent Butch down to capture the horse, while he went down in the gulch to find the dead sheep. Butch came back with the horse and said he had tied up the girl. After they removed the heads from the sheep, they put them in garbage bags, and loaded them on the horse. Then they went back to find the girl and decide what to do with her. The Boss said sometimes girls who went out riding had accidents.

"When they got to the place where Butch said he'd tied up the girl, she was gone. The Boss was very angry because he said he didn't want any witnesses. They looked around the area for the girl, but finally the Boss said they'd better get out of there. They went back to the truck, loaded up the heads, and took off."

"What kind of truck was Butch driving?"

"He had a big black Ford pickup with a crew cab."

"Did it have Colorado plates?"

"Yes, I think so. It had a gun rack in the back window."

"What happened to the horse?"

"They left it for someone to find."

"If you saw these guys in a line up, could you identify them?"

"Yes, I could."

"Can you think of anything else about them?"

"I don't think so."

The investigator reached over and turned off the recorder.

"Thank you. We might be contacting you again, so don't leave the area."

"I don't have any money, and we don't have anywhere else to go."

"Off the record, you were there, weren't you?"

"Yes, sir."

"But you never did any of the shooting?"

"No, sir."

"I know that you're very worried about the safety of your family. We'll try to keep you out of this if we can."

"Thank you, sir."

The investigator went back to the car where his partner was waiting.

"Did you do any good?"

"Jackpot! This guy Luis was there and saw the whole thing. He didn't do any of the shooting, but he's willing to identify the shooter and his partner."

"Shouldn't we grab this Luis guy?"

"No. Rutherfield is trying to arrange for immunity for him for testifying. According to Rutherfield, Luis had to make a choice between crossing the poachers and seeing his wife and kid get hurt, or going along with the poachers and seeing the witnesses get hurt."

"Found himself between the rock or the hard place."

"He decided to turn himself in, hoping the poachers would leave his family alone. When I showed up, he was convinced I was there to arrest him. Anyway, I've got his story on tape."

"Let's head over to the Kawuneeche Visitor Center where we can use one of their land lines to call this in and transfer your recording. They need to have this interview as soon as possible."

"Along the way, we need to keep watch for a black Ford crew cab pickup. According to Rutherfield, the poachers might be in the area to eliminate the witnesses."

———————————☞———————————

Back at Dante's Bar, Butch had another call from Tex.

"Why haven't you given me any information about the witnesses yet?"

"I have Luis Sandoval working on it."

"What! Do you mean to tell me you're leaving this assignment to that dumb Mexican?"

"First of all, he's not a Mexican. His ancestors were living in the San Luis Valley before the US was a country. He lives closer to Grand Lake than I do, so it's easier for him to check the place for information."

"Now you listen to me, and listen good. This is much too important to turn it over to this Luis guy, no matter where he's from. I gave you an assignment, and by damn if you know what's good for you, you'd better complete it... soon!"

Butch was rattled. "Who does Tex think he is anyway? No one talks to me that way," he said to himself. Then, after a few more bottles of Coors, he thought again about the incriminating evidence Tex might have on him. Tomorrow, he decided, I guess I'll have to make a trip to Grand Lake and snoop around.

Meanwhile, Tex did not sit back and have a few bottles of Coors. His preferred drink was Johnnie Walker Gold Label Reserve. He poured himself an unhealthy dose, and considered his options. It looked like Butch was not up to the job; he would have to take matters into his own hands. The next morning he was on the phone to 'YourJets' and made a reservation for a flight to Denver. One advantage of 'YourJets' was that there was no hassle about checking his luggage for weapons. Tex rented his preferred vehicle, a black SUV, and headed for Grand Lake.

Back in Colorado, Butch got in his truck and also headed for Grand Lake. It was normally about a two hour drive, but Butch was not in the mood to hurry. He stopped off at a feed store in Kremmling, picked up a tin of saddle soap, and asked the cashier if she had heard of any horse stealing lately. She said there was a rumor of someone stealing a horse over by Grand Lake, but didn't know anything about it.

Butch drove on to Grand Lake. As he approached the town, he stopped for gas at the Conoco station and filled up. He went in to pay and asked the clerk if he'd heard anything about horse stealing in the area lately. Jimmy, the clerk on duty, said there had been some rumors awhile back, but he didn't know anything about it. As Butch went back to his truck, Jimmy picked up the phone and called Amos.

"Hey, Amos. We just had a guy asking about horse stealing."

"What was he driving?"

"A black Ford pickup with a crew cab."

"Thanks for the tip, Jimmy."

The State Patrol agents who were still monitoring traffic, observed the truck.

"That pickup matches the description of one of the vehicles we're watching for."

"Let's follow him."

They got on the radio, reported the sighting, and that they were following the truck.

As soon as Amos got the call from Jimmy, he called Bill Rutherfield and let him know that a suspicious truck had been seen.

Butch drove on and stopped next at the general store. He purchased some jerky and an energy drink. Sue was at the register. Butch asked if she had heard anything about a stolen horse.

"Why do you ask? Did someone steal your horse?"

"Um, no. I just heard that there might be some horse thieves around."

Sue called to the back room.

"Hey, Jerry, come on out here. This fellow wants to know if anybody is stealing horses around here."

Jerry Peterson came out of his office and approached Butch.

"You the fella that's asking about horse thieves? If something like that is going on, we need to get the word out. Where are you from? If you give me your name and number, I sure will call you if I hear anything."

Butch mumbled, "I just heard some rumors and I was curious, that's all."

Butch went back to his truck. This might not be so easy, he thought to himself. He drove over to Lake Avenue near the boat docks and found a place where he could park overlooking the lake. He sat there for a while staring at the water, chewed on his jerky, sipped his drink, and silently muttered new curses at Tex.

As soon as Butch left the General Store, Jerry was on the phone to Amos.

"Hey Amos, it's Jerry. I think one of the bad guys is in town. He came asking about horse thieves. I played dumb, told him I'd let him know if I heard anything, and asked for his phone number, but he didn't bite. We do have a picture of him on our security camera though."

"Thanks Jerry, I'll pass the word along."

Meanwhile, the state patrol agents had followed the pickup truck, and were parked a block away from the truck where they could keep an eye on it. They reported in. The dispatcher reported back; they had information suggesting one of the poachers was in the truck, and that they should maintain surveillance until they got orders to move in.

Two state police patrol cruisers were dispatched to Grand Lake. One of them took up a position on the end of Lake Avenue opposite the unmarked car; the other turned on his flashers and stopped beside Butch's truck.

One officer approached the truck while the other took up a position with his hand on his weapon.

"Please step out of your vehicle, sir."

"What is this about, officer?"

The second cruiser approached from the other direction with lights flashing.

"You don't have any call to do this."

"We have a report that you were observed shoplifting from the general store. Now step out and show some identification... now, please!"

For a brief moment, Butch though about putting the truck in gear and making a run for it. Then he saw the second patrol car and gave up the idea. He got out of the truck and handed his driver's license to the officer.

"This is wrong. I ain't never shoplifted. You go and ask the man at the store."

"This will all be sorted out soon. Just come with us, please."

Butch was handcuffed, and put in the patrol car.

Since there was no State Patrol facility nearby, Butch was transported to the Grand County Jail in Hot Sulphur Springs. Bill Rutherfield had kept the County Sheriff's department informed about the poaching task force. The arresting officers radioed ahead, and the Sheriff was waiting for Butch in Hot Sulphur Springs.

Butch was finger printed, put in a cell, and the finger prints were faxed to a lab in Denver. They found a match with one of the prints on Starburst's saddle.

The Sheriff spoke to Butch through the cell bars.

"You got yourself in a heap of trouble, boy. You're going to be charged with killing sheep in Rocky Mountain National Park, and that's a federal offense. Worse than that, you're going to be charged with kidnapping. That's even worse than poaching sheep. You best be thinking what you're going to say when the Feds come to talk to you."

Bill faxed the information to the team. He called Amos and let him know about the arrest.

"One down, and one to go. We need to get a positive ID from Luis, but there is no question Butch Brown is one of the poachers. Maybe we can convince him to tell us about the guy he calls Boss."

## Chapter 22 - Danger in the Valley

When the first State Patrol special investigations unit was at the Kawuneeche Visitor Center transferring the recording of the Luis interview, and while the second unit was following Butch, no one was monitoring traffic into Grand Lake, and Tex breezed into town.

Tex had a different approach for identifying witnesses than the one tried by Butch. He drove around town observing bars and restaurants with signs in the window advertising some brand of alcohol. He was looking for the lowest class bar he could find. He finally decided that the Tumble Weed Bar and Grill was the most likely candidate for his scheme.

He parked his SUV where he could watch the front entrance to the bar, and settled in to observe customers coming and going. He focused on older unkempt single men. After several men who met his requirements entered the bar, Tex went in and found a booth that provided a good view of the customers. A waitress came over and took his order: a steak burger and a beer.

Tex watched and listened for a while. He focused in on one man who had apparently reached his capacity for booze. He had been bragging about his past exploits to anyone who would listen. Eventually, the bartender told him to leave since he couldn't pay for his drinks. The guy put up a fuss about this until the bartender finally said, "Come on, Jake, you've had enough now. Get yourself out of here or I'll have you thrown out physically."

This finally got Jake moving toward the door. Tex followed him out.

"Hey, pardner, It looks like they gave you the bum's rush. You still thirsty?"

"I'm always thirsty."

"I have a bottle of good stuff in my car, would you like a sip or two?"

"Mister, that's the kind of offer I never refuse."

Tex led Jake to his SUV and said, "Why don't you sit a spell? I heard you talking in the bar back there. You seem to have some interesting stories to tell."

Tex pulled out a bottle of cheap whiskey, poured some into a mug and handed it to Jake.

"Why, thank you, sir. I can tell you stories about this area that would curl your toenails."

"Do you know any stories about horse thieves?"

"Well.. let me think on that." He pushed the mug toward Tex, who added a little more whiskey.

"Ya know, back in the old days, they hanged horse thieves. As a matter of fact, when the mines were active around here, stealing as little as a shovel or pick ax might get a man hung. To the prospectors, a shovel or a gold pan was just about as important as a horse. In those days, there weren't no sheriff to call on, so the local boys took care of those things themselves."

Jake motioned for another refill. Tex poured a little more into the mug.

"How about lately? Any horse thieves still around?"

"Well, as a matter of fact, there was a strange one. That girl Jane who works up at Elk Park Ranch had her horse stolen. Funny thing was the thief just went and left the horse behind the general store."

"What about this Jane, didn't she try to stop the thief?"

"Well, as I understand it, the thief jumped her and hogtied her."

"How'd she get away?"

"Some photographer fella was hiking by and let her loose"

"Sounds like a real hero. What's his story? Is he a local man?"

"I heard his name is Andrew and he was just travelin' through. Think he's stayin' at the same ranch where the girl works."

Tex had heard enough. He switched from the bottle of cheap whiskey to a smaller hip flask he had laced with Librium, and refilled the mug again. He coached Jake to tell him more about hanging in the old days.

"Well, probly the most famous person who was hanged was Jack Slade. He used to operate stage stops for the Overland Stage Company…."

Jake finally dozed off. Tex made sure no one was watching, dragged him out of the SUV, and leaned him up against a trash can. He thought to himself, "that was easier than I expected." Now he had both names and a location. He took out the copy of the Grand County Visitors Guide he had picked up earlier, and found directions to Elk Park Ranch.

Tex spent some time scouting out the area around the Elk Park Ranch, and located a small hill with a clear view of the ranch. Now he had to somehow find a way to identify Jane and her rescuer.

He drove to Winter Park, bought a knitted scarf and a hat, and then went to the local print shop that had a UPS sign in the window. Putting the scarf and hat into different UPS mailers, he addressed one to Jane, Elk Park Ranch, Grand Lake, Colorado, and the other to Andrew. He put a bogus return address on the packages.

He asked the clerk how long it would take the packages to be delivered, and was told for an extra fee he could get service with guaranteed delivery by noon the next day. He paid cash, then checked in for the night at a Winter Park Motel.

He got up at daybreak the next day, drove back to Grand Lake, parked at the Green Mountain trail head, and waited until there was no traffic. He then slipped across Route 34 to the west side of the road. Once he was hidden in the timber, he took his camo gear out of his back pack, put it on, and made his way to a vantage point with a view of the office entrance. He set up his Blaser R93 and waited.

A little after noon, a UPS truck appeared. The driver delivered two packages to the office, and drove off. Tex watched several people enter and leave the office, none carrying a package. Finally a man and a woman entered the office and came out, each holding a UPS package. Tex decided to go for a head shot for the woman first, then pick off the man. The range was 500 yards, a little longer than the big horn sheep shot, but well within the range of the Blaser R93.

Tex aimed at Jane's head and squeezed the trigger.

The bright high altitude sunlight had been shining on the Kawuneeche Valley all morning. The warming air rose up and was replaced by cool air falling down from the peaks of the Never Summer mountains creating a mild breeze across the valley. The breeze caused the 500 yard long shot from the Blaser R93 to miss Jane's head by two inches. It smashed the glass in the front door of the office. Andrew immediately pulled Jane down behind a planter as a second bullet exploded a chunk of wood from the wall behind where Andrew had been standing.

"Keep down!" Andrew said to Jane. "Someone's shooting at us."

"But I didn't hear any shot," Jane exclaimed.

"I didn't hear any shot when the sheep were killed either. But the glass in the door didn't break itself."

Marge had heard the door glass breaking and opened the door.

"What happened?"

Andrew shouted, "There's a sniper shooting at us. Call the state patrol!"

Andrew peeked through the flowers in the planter and tried to guess where the shots had come from. There was no one in sight. The only possible place for the shooter to hide was a low hill across the meadow to the north of the ranch.

"When I say go, let's dash around the side of the building. Now. Go!"

They made it.

"I think we're safe as long as we're out of sight of that hill over there. Let's move around to the kitchen door, and get inside."

"I called the state patrol," Marge reported. "They'll send a cruiser as soon as possible, but they don't have anyone close right now."

"Do you have ranger Bob's number?"

"I have it," Jane offered.

"Call him, and then let me talk to him."

Jane made the call, told Bob they had been shot at, and then handed the phone to Andrew,.

"Hi, Bob, this is Andrew. Someone just took a couple of shots at us when were in front of the Elk Park Ranch office. The front door glass was shattered, and a second shot took a big chunk out of the wall beside the door. As far as I can tell, the shooter must have been on the small hill across the valley to the north of the ranch."

"How long ago did this happen?"

"Less then five minutes ago."

"If the shooter was on that hill, he had to have come in from the highway somewhere. I'm going to set up a road block and check every vehicle leaving the area."

Bob made quick calls to Bill Rutherfield, and the state patrol. He shouted down the hall to Joe, "It looks like the poacher just took a shot at Jane and Andrew. Grab your weapon and let's go!"

As they jumped into their NPS Chevy Blazer, Bob gave Joe a quick review of his phone call from Andrew.

"Unless he came in on horseback, the only way out is through Grand Lake, or up over Trail Ridge Road." Bob said.

"My bet is that he won't head over Trail Ridge. It's too slow."

"If he came in on horseback, we're going to have a problem."

"If we don't find his vehicle, we'll have to call in an air search."

"If he drove in, he had to park his car somewhere close to Elk Park Ranch. Let's check the Green Mountain trail head parking lot."

As soon as Tex fired the shots, he saw Jane and Andrew go down. He was not sure, however, if they'd been hit. In any case, they were not in view, and he had to get out of the area... and fast. He broke down the Blaser R93, put it back in it's case, and put the case in his back pack. He then made his way back toward the SUV.

As he came to the point where he had to cross Route 34, he looked both ways to make sure the road was empty. He almost made it across as Bob and Joe came speeding around a curve and up the road. Tex went to his car, and tried to pretend he was a regular hiker as Bob and Joe pulled up.

"Howdy, rangers," Tex said, "Nice day for a hike."

Tex reached into his back pack and got his hand on his Colt Peacemaker. Bob and Joe spread out and put their hands on their weapons as they approached.

"The hiking trails are all on this side of the road, here, and you just came across from the other side. We need to see some ID."

Tex protested, "You have no right to be harassing a hiker and asking for an ID. I think you better find somebody else to bother."

"We can tag you for hiking off trail without a permit. Now take your hand out of that backpack and let's see some ID."

Tex pulled his Colt out of the backpack. As he made that move, Bob and Joe pulled out their service weapons.

Bob said, "Unless you want to leave here in a box, you better put that antique away."

Tex didn't have the guts for an old fashioned shootout. He slowly lowered the Colt and dropped it to the ground. Bob kept him covered while Joe handcuffed him. They locked Tex in the back seat of their Blazer, and searched his backpack. Opening the Blaser R93 case, Bob sniffed the barrel and noted that the gun had been fired recently. They also checked Tex's ID.

Bob grinned, "It looks like we found our poacher. If ballistics can match this rifle with the bullet we took from the sheep, this guy is toast."

"We can also get him for attempted murder. Let's send our crew over to that hill overlooking the Elk Park Ranch and see if they can find a couple of casings."

"What do you want to do about his SUV?"

"Let's have it impounded. By the time he gets out, even if a clever lawyer can post his bail, he'll have some serious storage fees and overdue rental fees."

"I love it."

Bob and Joe drove back to the Kawuneeche Visitor Center. Tex was locked in their Blazer with Joe on guard while Bob went in and made several calls. The first was to Bill Rutherfield.

"We just caught the poacher red-handed with a Blaser R93 smelling like it has been recently fired. It looks like we might have the poacher case wrapped up."

Bob told Bill as much as he knew about the shooting, and the capture of Tex.

"The shooter is Dr. Moses Frey of Wichita Falls, Texas. Apparently he goes by Tex. When we caught him, he was in possession of a Blaser R93. He also had a Colt Peacemaker that he pulled on us when we caught up to him. We talked him out of playing OK corral with it. Real soon now he'll be on his way to the Grand County jail. We're heading there as soon as I hang up."

Bill chuckled, "He and his friend Butch Brown will be having a poacher's reunion there. The Sheriff convinced Butch to 'get religion' and it looks like there's no honor among poachers. I've arranged for a raid on Rob Role's taxidermy shop. It's likely the two ram heads are still there. Max Smith, our Alamosa game warden, has been suspicious about that shop for awhile. It looks like this will close down the Manassa operation. Unfortunately, we don't have a line on any of Tex Frey's customers yet. If we're lucky, he might have kept records.

Thanks for your fast action capturing Tex. Thank heavens I no longer have to worry about Jane. I felt a little guilty putting her in a dangerous situation when I asked her to look around for poachers."

Bob tried to console Bill, "I don't think you're responsible for putting her in danger. She wasn't chasing poachers when they caught her sunbathing. By the way, I'm thinking about offering her a job here as a naturalist with the National Park Service. I sent up a trial balloon to get her thinking about it. We have someone retiring, and I can tailor a job opening for her if she wants it."

"That's good to hear. I hope she takes advantage of your offer. It's time she gets into something more permanent, and something more in line with her education and interests. Thanks for your call. I need to finalize the details to wrap up this case."

Andrew and Jane had gone back to her cabin after the phone call to Bob. Jane suddenly started shivering and sat on the bed."

Andrew put his arms around Jane, "Are you OK?"

"I was just realizing the bullet that hit the porch door probably came within a couple of inches of my head."

"I've been thinking the same thing. We just have to remember we're both OK now, and try not to dwell on what might have happened."

"Inside somewhere I know that. But still…" Jane hugged Andrew closer.

## Chapter 23 - Case Closed

The next day was the 4th of July. The Elk Park Ranch group gathered in the Green Mountain Room for the breakfast buffet.

Ned was telling the others about Luis and Starburst, "I asked Luis to exercise Starburst and I warned him how Starburst was skittish around strangers. When Luis approached Starburst, it was the strangest thing. Starburst came right up to him and nuzzled him like they were old friends. I think Luis might be some kind of horse whisperer."

Jane gave Luis a wink.

Nancy added, "Maria is fitting in as though she's been working here a long time."

Maria responded, "It's easy to make friends with friendly people. You don't know how much you people have helped Luis and me when we really needed help."

Mary was showing off her latest drawings to Andrew, who was making a proper fuss over them.

After breakfast, Jane and
Andrew wandered over to the
corral, leaned on the fence,
and gazed across the meadow
to the Never Summer
Mountains.

"Do you think after
spending years working in New York City, you could
ever be happy working on a newspaper in a little town
like Grand Lake"?

"I think I could, especially if I had a beautiful
naturalist to share my life with. Do you think someday
we might call 'Aunt Martha' and make a proper
married couple reservation at the Drowsy Creek
Lodge?"

Jane smiled and took both Andrew's hands, "If
that's a proposal, it sounds like a good plan to me."

"Well, it's a very serious proposal. What do you
say?"

Jane hugged Andrew around the neck, gave him a
big kiss, and replied, "I say yes!"

After more hugging and kissing, Jane asked,
"Have you forgotten about Arvid's treasure?"

"No, but there have been too many other things to
think about. How would you like to take a hike?"

"Do you really expect to find treasure?"

"One never knows."

———————————————☞———————————————

Andrew and Jane hiked back to the place where he had pitched his tent, and where he and Jane had crowded into his sleeping bag.

Andrew showed Jane Arvid's map, "There must be some reason why Arvid made this mark here."

"Do you know what the mark means?"

"When I was doing some research in the New York Public Library, I discovered an article on ancient viking runes. The rune that looks like the mark on Arvid's map is translated as *inheritance,* or *heritage.*"

"Do you think Arvid left something to be inherited?"

"Could be. Let's look around to see if we can find the mark. Let's start here and make expanding circles.

Andrew moved off clockwise from the tent site, while Jane moved counter clockwise. Up against a steep outcrop, Andrew saw an area that looked like it was blackened with smoke. Near the bottom of the smoked area was what looked like slag. It reminded him of pictures he had seen of ancient Scandinavian bank furnaces. He knew Arvid had worked for a blacksmith back in Sweden and possibly learned about bank furnaces; perhaps this is where Arvid had created the silver ingot. Near the blackened stones, he found an arrow carved into a rock.

Jane cried out, "Look over here; this looks like an arrow pointing in that direction."

"I was just going to tell you that I found an arrow over there, but it's pointing in a different direction. If we can find another arrow maybe they all point to a single spot, like this."

Andrew fished a pencil out of his back pack and drew a sketch on the back of the map.

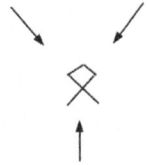

They searched in the general direction to which the two arrows were pointing. Jane shouted, "I think I found the third arrow."

"Excellent. Now let's see if we can find what they are pointing to."

Andrew wished he had brought along some string; then he could stretch strings following the different arrow directions. That would make the search easier. He picked up small stones and created lines following the direction of one of the arrows; Jane saw what he was doing and did the same thing from her arrow. Andrew made a line of stones from the third arrow. It soon became obvious where the three lines met.

Andrew knelt down, scraped the fallen pine needles away from the area, and discovered a flat stone about a foot across.

"This must be it!"

Jane held her breath while Andrew lifted the stone and found a small tin box similar to the one Arvid had sent east nearly a hundred years before.

With difficulty, Andrew opened the box and emptied the contents on the unfolded map. There was a small silver ingot like the one Arvid had sent to his family, a number of coins, several Swedish Kroner, 20 Morgan dollars, several mining claim papers, and one scrap of paper with crude writing:

> Jag kan inte bli rik genom
> att gräva.
> Jag måste sälja papper.

"What does that mean?"

"It's in Swedish. I know very little Swedish. The only thing I can make out is *Jag kan inte* which means I cannot. We need a Swedish English dictionary."

"At least you've done the impossible. You've found Arvid's treasure, but it doesn't look like it will make you rich."

"Actually, I did find a treasure on this trip. One much better than what Arvid buried."

"What do you mean? What treasure did you find?"

"I'm looking at her."

By the time they made the hike back to the ranch, they were exhausted. Jane said she needed a shower. Andrew asked if she needed someone to scrub her back. She smiled, but didn't say no.

———————————————☟———————————————

On Monday, Bill Rutherfield was presiding over a meeting of the task force.

"The big horn poaching incident has been resolved. We have clear ballistic evidence showing the bullet taken from the sheep body came from the Blaser R93 found in Tex Frey's possession. Butch Brown has been singing like a Lark Bunting. We also have a second eye witness, Luis Sandoval. We've received immunity for Sandoval for his assistance in breaking the case.

"Rob Role's taxidermy shop was raided, and he was still in possession of two big horn ram heads. Forensic analysis confirms that the heads match the sheep bodies recovered from RMNP. Rob Role is permanently out of the taxidermy business.

"There's no question Dr. Tex Frey will be convicted for poaching big game from a National Park.

The charges of attempted murder, however, are complicated. We have recovered cartridges from where Tex fired shots at Jane and Andrew; we have the weapon used, and we have recovered matching bullets. The problem is one of jurisdiction. It turns out that Frey was on RMNP property when the shots were fired. However, the intended victims were on private property, just outside the Park boundary. The lawyers and judges will have fun fighting that out.

"The Texas Rangers raided Tex Frey's office and home. They found records with names of customers, the trophy sold, and the amount paid. By analyzing bones and teeth from the mounted heads, forensic experts will probably be able to determine where the animals lived. This information will result in confiscation of trophy heads and some very stiff fines.

"I want to thank you all for your efforts in this case. I think by the time all is said and done, we will have solved a lot more than just the case of the big horn poaching."

---

Meanwhile, back at the ranch, a celebration of sorts was underway. Several tables had been pushed together to make one large table where a group was assembled. The group consisted of the ranch staff: Marge, Ned, Jane, Luis, and Maria. It had been announced earlier that Luis and Maria had been hired. Nancy had been recruited to babysit for Mary in the Sandoval's cabin, where she was showing Mary how to draw a big horn sheep. Andrew and Amos Shipler were the two non-ranch staff members in the group.

Marge called for attention, "I have some bad news and some good news. The bad news is that Jane has decided to resign from her job here at Elk Park Ranch. The good news is that she's taken a job as a naturalist with the National Park Service. She'll be working at the Kawuneeche Visitor Center and, for a while at least, she'll continue to live in her cabin here on the ranch."

Amos Shipler then said, "I have only good news. Andrew has agreed to join the staff of the Grand Lake Spectator. I'm very confident that he'll be an excellent addition to our newspaper and to the Grand Lake community."

Marge added, "Some more good news is the ranch will soon be hosting Andrew and Jane's wedding."

In Basking Ridge, New Jersey, Annie Olofsson was removing a batch of chocolate chip cookies from the oven when she heard her neighbor Martha call through the screen door, "Those cookies smell good. Is the coffee ready?"

"Just come in and help yourself as you always do. I don't know why you even ask."

"I'm just pretending to be polite. Have you heard anything from your nephew lately?"

"Yes, yesterday I got a long letter from him."

"Has he had those big adventures you sent him off to find?"

"Yes, he has. In the first place, he found out what happened to Uncle Arvid."

"What happened?"

"It turns out that Arvid was killed in a train wreck in Iowa. Andrew even saw Arvid's grave."

"How on earth did Andrew find Arvid's grave in Iowa?"

"When they were building the first train track through Iowa, they built over a section of unstable ground. Because of the unstable ground, a bridge collapsed under a train and many people were killed. That part of the train track is still unstable, and when Andrew's train came through, it had to stop because a freight train wrecked in the same place. Andrew's train was held up for several days while the track was being repaired. Well, Andrew didn't have much to do while waiting for the track to be fixed, so he went to a local museum and learned about the old train wreck. A display had a copy of an old newspaper account of the wreck, and it mentioned Arvid's name."

"That's incredible. Did Andrew ever find the lost mine?"

"It turns out there was no mine. Andrew followed Arvid's map and discovered a buried tin box similar to the one Arvid sent here. The box had a few coins, another little silver ingot, some mining claim papers, and a note."

"What did the note say?"

"It was in Swedish. It said:

> Jag kan inte bli rik genom
> att gräva.
> Jag måste sälja papper."

"What does that mean?"."

"It means *I can't get rich by digging; I have to sell paper.* Apparently Arvid was coming back east to sell mine claims to investors. That was a very common practice in those days. I remember reading about that in Mark Twain's book Roughing It."

"You sent Andrew chasing after Arvid's treasure in hopes he would get out of his job loss funk and have some adventures. How did that work out?"

"Well, Andrew saved a girl from kidnappers, rescued a mother and daughter from a flood, and got shot at by a sniper."

"I think that certainly qualifies as having adventures. So, is Andrew coming back soon?"

"I don't think so. He decided to take a job with a small Colorado newspaper."

"I guess maybe he found himself then."

"He found more than that."

"What do you mean?"

"He found the right girl, and he's going to get married."

"Well Annie, I guess your pushing Andrew turned out for the best."

"That's what aunts are for."

## About the Author

please visit http://lenshamn.com/about_14/about_len.html

## Books related to this story;
## Available on Amazon

**Mark Twain**, *Roughing It*

**Tom Brown Jr.**, *The Tracker: The True Story of Tom Brown Jr.*

**Caroline Bancroft**, *Unique Ghost Towns and Mountain Spots*

**Isabella Bird**, *A Lady's Life in the Rocky Mountains*

**Stephen E. Ambrose**, *The Men Who Built the Transcontinental Railroad*

**C. W. Bucholtz**, *Rocky Mountain National Park: A History*

**Erik Stensland**, *Hiking Rocky Mountain National Park: The Essential Guide*

**Troy Nesbit**, Sand Dune Pony

## Author's note:

The story of Arvid's treasure is fiction. However, the historical references and *most* of the locations described are real.

Made in the USA
Coppell, TX
04 January 2021

47517842R00174